Hanna

The President's Daughter

Hanna, The President's Daughter
Copyright © John Denison, 2011
All rights reserved, including the right of
reproduction in whole or in part in any form.

This is a work of fiction. Names, characters, places and
incidents are either a product of the author's imagination
or used fictitiously. Any resemblance to actual persons,
living or dead, events, or locales is entirely coincidental.

ISBN (book): 978-0-9877788-5-7
ISBN (e-book): 978-0-9877788-6-4

CIP available

Cover image: Jy Chiperzak
Cover & book design: Gill Stead
Inside (p173) and back cover photographs courtesy of Shutterstock

Why Knot Books
5443 Eighth Line,
Erin, ON, N0B 1T0
Canada
Editorial: 519-833-1242
Distribution: Jason Dickson, 705-646-2215

Hanna

The President's Daughter

JOHN DENISON

WHY KNOT BOOKS

Will CADIE herself at some point connect her own electromagnetic dots in some idiosyncratic manner which turns into something we are no longer capable of understanding in any sort of productive way, much as that aforementioned toddler, waving at herself in the mirror, leaves primates forever behind in their own tragically limited world?

We don't know. Did you really think we possibly could?

The CADIE Team, March 31, 2009

1

The Unhappy President

After fifteen years I know when my dad's pissed at me. He doesn't look me in the eyes. He looks past me, around me, behind me, below me, till he's ready to do battle. Then he zeroes in like a deer hunter with a laser scope.

Tonight's different because I don't know *why* he's pissed. I mean you know when you've been dumb, right? *Man, if they find out I'm doing this I'm going to be in serious doo-doo.* That kind of thing. I mean, really, I don't figure a daughter's doing her job if she doesn't make her parents ballistic once in a while.

But I'm also an A student; I play on the volleyball team; I'm still a virgin; I don't smoke; I don't do drugs; and I'm nice to my little brother. Things could be worse, right?

So why the President's miffed I haven't a clue.

Tonight we're eating in the President's Dining Room on the second floor. The top two floors of the White House are our *private* living quarters but the only thing private about them is they're not on the tour. This is usually where we eat when the President of the United States isn't entertaining the Queen of Denmark or the Prime Minister of New Zealand.

Sometimes Michael, my ten-year-old brother, and I are invited to these lavish State Dinners but mostly we're not which suits us fine. On those days we usually pig-out in the kitchen with Chef Henri.

"Hanna."

Here we go. Mr. President, a.k.a. Dad, is lining me up in his sights and his finger is squeezing the trigger.

"Yes, Mr. President?"

Calling Dad *Mr. President* is guaranteed to double the number of bullets coming my way.

The 45th President of the United States picks up the magazine that is lying face down on the table beside him and holds it up for me to see. It's the new *People* magazine and – oh wow! – I'm on the cover! And – oh wow! – I'm wearing my frayed, blue jean short-shorts with bare feet and my bright red tank top, the one that says, in big white letters, *Lisbeth Kicks Ass*. Bra strap. Bit of cleavage – bit's all I've got! – but nothing to flip out about.

And – oh yeah – that's Jason with his arm resting on my shoulder.

Jason and I are friends. He's gay but I'm the only one who knows except his mom and Jen. I'll admit it might have been better if Jason had been wearing a shirt – but at least he's buff. He reminds me of Matt Damon playing Jason Bourne.

Mr. President hands the magazine to the First Lady, a.k.a. Mom. She knows better than to smile. Instead she pretends to study the photo.

"I wanna see," says Michael and the First Lady passes him the magazine. Now she's the one who won't look at me. But I can see her lips twitching so I know she wants to burst out laughing. "Am I in here too?" Michael asks flipping through the pages.

As usual no one answers Michael. Of the 10,000 questions he's asked since birth at least 7,500 have gone unanswered.

No one says anything. I pick up my hamburger and take another bite. Organic beef, organic multigrain bun, organic tomato, organic sweet potato fries, organic greens, even organic ketchup. Organic milk. The First Lady's from California and firmly believes you are what you eat.

At the moment she's on a crusade to change America's Eating

Habits. So far the steroid-antibiotic-cut-down-the-rainforest burgers from FastFoodLand are winning but we'll see. My mother the supermodel, for all her looks, can be a scrapper. I'm betting on Mom.

"Hanna, you are the President's daughter." I look over my bun at The Most Powerful Man in the World. "You cannot march around wearing no clothes, especially clothes that say *Lisbeth Kicks Ass.*"

I wait.

"Who the hell is Lisbeth anyway?"

"Lisbeth Salander – she's the hero of some books I like. *The Girl with the Dragon Tattoo* is the first. You should read them."

I can see the President digesting this information. I figure he'd rather do battle with the Joint Chiefs of Staff than have to make sense of his daughter.

"And who's this *boy*?" The word *boy* is said in the same tone as you'd say *dogshit* just after you stepped in it.

"That's my friend Jason." One of my strategies is to answer all questions but never say more than necessary. I find it drives adults bonkers and that's what teenagers are for, right?

The President looks to the First Lady for Help. Mom tries her best.

"Hanna, we're not everyday citizens any more. We're under a microscope. Everything we do is talked about. How you and I and Michael act reflects on your dad. It's important that we set a good example. Your father has enough problems at the moment without us adding to them."

Now our eyes are locked together. She continues: "There's nothing wrong with that photo. You look wonderful. Jason looks great. But together you look like you're getting ready to make love on the beach and for the fifteen-year-old daughter of the President that's not setting a good example."

Ouch. I can feel tears starting but then I remember Lisbeth Salander and send the tears back where they came from. All eyes are on me and finally I nod. Wait till they find out I designed that tank top and it's selling like *crazy* on Threadless.

Dad, of course, can't let it go. He uses one of his good ol' boy voices and says: "Mr. President, if you can't control your own daughter, how do you expect-"

"Hold it."

That's me saying *hold it*. "*Control* your daughter?" I'm losing it now. "Is that what you want? To *control* me?"

The President is taken aback. No one interrupts the President.

"Well, control's not the right word, but you're only fifteen for god's sake. Mac, help me here." He looks at my mom for reassurance. (Just in case you're from another planet I'll tell you my mom is that supermodel that everybody calls Mac because her real name is Mackenzie. She's very tall and very beautiful and very smart like in savvy.)

"Sorry Mr. President, I'm with Hanna on this one."

Things are quiet after that. Michael wants to know why he isn't in the magazine and Mom says he will be just you wait and see. Finally I take pity on the President. I'm smart enough to see things from my parents' point of view and I can see how I might drive you to drink now and again. Besides, there's something I want.

"I'm sorry about the photo. Now, Mr. President, why don't you tell us what's really bothering you?"

The President stares at me, then he turns to the First Lady, then he comes back to me.

"You're something Hanna, you know that?" Then he starts into one of his rants – this one about paid lobbyists.

"Do you know who lobbyists are Hanna?"

"Yep, they're paid to represent Special Interest Groups in Washington. In the old days they hung out in the Congressional lobby. That's where the name came from. They were sometimes called the third house. Some of the early lobbyists were women and they were said to be most effective."

I say women in such a way that it means they were willing to shed their clothes to get what they wanted.

"I'm impressed."

Here's where I should give my history teacher, Miss Longbottom, credit but I don't. I don't like her and she doesn't like me.

"What's a specialinterestgroup?" Michael asks through a mouthful of burger.

"Say there is a company that makes lots of money catching tuna," – Mom is good at using examples that Michael will relate to – "and say everybody thinks they're catching too many tuna."

"So many tuna that someday there won't be any," adds Dad.

"Tragedy of the Commons," I put in and it's something else I've learned in history class. It means when you have a common resource like the fish in the ocean no one takes responsibility for those fish. Everybody just catches as many fish as they can and too bad if someday there are no fish to catch.

Michael says, "Bluefin tuna is on the endangered species list."

"That's right. So people don't want tuna to disappear so they want the government, your dad, to pass a law saying you can only catch this many tuna."

"Which is common sense," says me, "and the basis of sustainability which should be the bottom line of everything."

"Amen," says the President.

"But," Mom continues, "the people who make money catching tuna – they're the Special Interest Group – they don't want a law passed telling them how many fish they can catch so they pay these men and women called lobbyists to talk to the Congressmen and Senators and make sure they don't vote for any laws that would limit their fishing."

"That's stupid," Michael says.

Dad grins at this. "Mark was telling me that all together lobbyists get paid 10 million dollars *a day* to make sure their Special Interest Groups are looked after."

"That's a lot of tuna," says the First Lady.

Michael loves fish. That's why Mom used tuna as an example. Right now I'm following Michael to his bedroom because he has something to show me. The President's gone back to work and the First Lady has gone to answer her email. Michael's next door to me in the West Bedroom. When Theodore Roosevelt was President his ten-year-old son Archie had this room and once when he was sick his younger brother Quentin brought Archie's pony – Algonquin – up in the elevator to visit him. I mean this place is dripping with history.

Before you move into the White House – it's called that because it's made of porous sandstone that won't last unless it's whitewashed – Mrs. Brown, the Curator, asks you what you'd like in your room. She has these photo binders full of furniture and paintings – old museum stuff that's sitting in storage somewhere. Michael picked out a four-poster bed Willie Lincoln slept and died in and a big desk John F. Kennedy used.

When it was my turn I pointed at this set of old wooden plywood stuff that looked like it should have gone to the dump years ago but it reminded me of the falling apart stuff at my camp and I love camp. I got a desk with a drawer that won't open and a weird kind of half drawers/half mirror thing that I use for make-up, and a double bed with initials carved in it – BK loves TK – two comfy wicker chairs and a round table with twig legs.

I mean it's all totally inappropriate for the White House but I think that's why I like it. Think you're hot stuff cuz your dad's President? – think again. That's what I say now. The day I picked it out I was in such a bitchy mood. I just wanted to freak out Mrs. Brown but you got to love her. She says, "Hanna, I think you're going to be a lot of fun. Let's do it!"

Now we're in Michael's bedroom which is the same size and layout as mine. He doesn't turn the lights on because he has all these fish tanks with moonlights. The place glows. It's like walking into an underwater cave.

He has like eight big tanks all at different levels, all hooked together with clear plastic pipe big enough for the fish to swim through. The tanks are sealed at the top so the water doesn't overflow. All except the top tank which is open so Michael can add water or fish or food. He has to climb a stepladder to do that.

What's cool is one of the pipes goes through the closet hall into my bedroom and runs along the wall above my desk. So like you're sitting there trying to do your homework and all of a sudden this bright yellow fish whips by with one of those phosphorescent blue guys right on his tail. For some reason the fish going by always makes me laugh.

"You gotta see this," Michael says. "This is way cool." We're staring into a large tank off to the side that Michael says is for breeding. This tank isn't connected to the other tanks and swimming around inside are a pair of the funniest looking fish, about the size of my hand with this back fin thing that looks like this < .

They're a dark browny-black color with white vertical stripes just before the tail starts but what's really funny is they have this nose that looks like something out of Pinocchio.

"What kind of fish are these?" I ask.

"Peters' Elephant Nose fish." Okay, so not Pinocchio, an elephant's trunk. "The trunk is their bottom lip," Michael says. "They use it to find food in the dirt."

"Where are they from?"

"The Niger River in Africa."

"That's cool. What are you doing with them?"

"I'm going to breed them."

It suddenly occurs to me that I have no idea how fish mate. I know about people, dogs, whales and moose but fish-

"How exactly do they do that?"

"The female lays eggs and the male fertilizes them."

There you go. "Then what?"

"Then I'll be famous."

"Because?"

"They've never bred in captivity before."

"You're kidding?"

"Nope," Michael says. "This will be the first time."

"Wow, I'm impressed." And I am impressed. Michael's a pretty cool kid. "You know you're already famous."

"Mom and Dad are famous, we're just appendages."

Only Michael would say *appendages*. But he's right. We're like barnacles on the Ship of State. See, I can be poetic too.

"So, what are their names," I ask.

"Wendy and Wayne." Cute.

"Okay, soon-to-be-famous boy, gotta go do homework."

I leave little brother staring at *Michael World*.

2

Miss Eleanor Longbottom

I go to Bidwell Friends School. I'm at the high school and Michael's in the middle school. Bidwell is a Quaker School where all the presidents' kids have gone. Best school in Washington they say. Certainly has the tightest security but that's mostly Michael's and my fault I guess. No one wants a President's kid to be kidnapped – me included.

Anyway, Bidwell is okay. I've already made two good friends, Jason and Jen, and I'm okay with my teachers except my history teacher Miss Eleanor Longbottom. Really. Would you so not change your name? We all call her Neville after the character in the Harry Potter books.

And she's Miss not Ms and I swear she can't be more than twenty-two years old. She's petite but there's something military about her – could be the short dirty blonde hair – so I keep seeing her as Hitler's niece or something. Face-wise she looks like a ferret but if I liked her she'd get pixyish. And she's from England so she's got this accent which I want to say grates me but it's actually kind of pleasant, but I can't admit that right?

Here's my theory: Miss Eleanor Longbottom (Neville) hates everybody cuz her name is Eleanor Longbottom, and me in particular because she's never going to be famous like the President's daughter.

Maybe she can sing like Adele but I wouldn't bet on it.

So today at the end of class she has this stack of envelopes with a name on each one. She hands them out and I'm last. She gives me this evil grin.

"These are your essay assignments. 2500 words. They're due a week from today. Every day you're late you'll lose 10%."

"How 'bout if we're early?" I blurt this out to maintain my role as *Class Disturber of Shit* though my mom always says go for the positive reward rather than the negative punishment. Neville ignores me.

We open our envelopes. I read mine and look up. Miss Longbottom is staring at me with this look on her face like she's just dumped a bucket of blood on my desk and what am I going to do about it?

I turn and walk out the door. I walk straight to the Principal's office and stand at the counter until Mrs. Shadwell looks up at me. Mrs. Shadwell's last makeover was in 1969.

"You don't look happy," she says.

"Could I see Ms. Black?" Ms. Black is the principal. She's fairly young and pretty cool. My mom wishes she could hire her.

"Go right in, I'm sure she'll be glad to see you."

Ms. Black is at her computer. Her glasses are resting at the end of her nose. She turns towards me and laughs.

"Hanna, you look like a storm cloud."

I hand her the envelope and she pulls the piece of paper out.

"Discuss the four Presidential assassinations and the impact on the families."

I can see Ms. Black thinking – picking her words.

"Miss Longbottom, right?" I nod. "You've had a couple of run-ins with her."

"Yes."

"You embarrassed her in class."

"She was wrong."

"We all make mistakes, Hanna."

"She's the teacher."

"As I understand it you were less than kind in correcting her."

She's right. Neville was expounding her theory that short men become conquerors to make up for their lack of height – just look at Napoleon and Hitler and Attila the Hun. So I interrupt and say that's wrong – none of those guys were short for the times.

Nonsense says Neville – Napoleon was five feet nothing. Wanta bet, says me. I know this stuff cuz I wrote an essay on height once. So we Google it and sure enough Napoleon is five foot seven or eight – Tom Cruise height and I'm like Nicole Kidman five eleven plus. Miss Longbottom turns bright red and if she's carrying a gun I'm dead. Buy hey, she was wrong, right?

(After Nicole K divorces Tom C she says *Thank god I can wear heels again*. And what about the irony of petite Miss Longbottom picking on not so petite Napoleon? I love irony!)

Ms. Black and I sit quietly for some seconds – long enough for Ms. Black's screensaver to come on. It's the Bidwell School crest – the one with the Latin motto: Vitam Vivere – Live Life.

"Miss Longbottom is very young and very bright," says Ms. Black finally. "This is her first teaching job. I think she's still nervous about the whole thing – especially in a high-powered class like yours."

I don't say anything. I can hear kids laughing outside the window, heading home.

"What you learn in school is important Hanna, but, the most important thing you learn is how to deal with other people. There will always be people you don't connect with, like Miss Longbottom. You have to learn to deal with her just as she has to learn to deal with you."

Ms. Black gives me time to think about this. "Would you like me to arrange a meeting with the three of us?"

I shake my head and leave.

That was a flashback to earlier today. Now I'm in my bedroom – the East Bedroom – Googling Presidential assassinations and get the four names: Lincoln, Garfield, McKinley and Kennedy and my first interesting fact which is after Lincoln was shot the new President was named Johnson and after Kennedy was shot the new President was named Johnson!

Then I'm interrupted by a text from Jason:
<were on the cover of people!!!!>
<the President wanted to know WHO U R?>
<im innocent!!>
<you had bisexual in your heart admit it!>
<no! that was mayo!>
<i told him we couldnt do it cuz of the SS>
<didnt!>
<didnt – you'd better come over and meet him>
<he's scary where'd you go today?>
<neville pissed me off>
<join the club what did you get?>
<presidential assassinations>
<that stinks did you tell your dad?>
<nope what did you get>
<explain americas role in afghanistan>
<good luck with that – jen?>
<why is america always at war>
<ouch – mines easier than those two>
<when should I meet the big P?>

Now my screen dissolves and Roadrunner comes barrelling across the screen screeching to a halt in a cloud of dust. "Beep, beep." That's code for Yingyang wants to see me.

<gotta go syt>

Yingyang is this cool guy who looks after the computers in the WH.

He's thirty-two and a genius. His real name is Yuien but everybody calls him Yingyang. His dad is African-American and his mom is Vietnamese. My dad gave me a MacBook Air for all the work I did during the election – social networking y'know – and Yingyang's been teaching me all the stuff it can do.

I make my way down to the White House Ground Floor where Yingyang has his office. Half the office is tidy and the other half looks like a bomb went off. Yingyang's definitely a Gemini. He's sitting in front of his Mac on the tidy side. Without looking to see who it is he holds up a copy of *the* magazine.

"Nice legs."

"Me or Jason?"

"You have like 30,000 emails. Most of them from young males with sticky fingers."

"You're kidding, right?"

"U R like so awesome. Marry me and we'll run away to Thailand. I have $$$ saved. We're good for 5 or 6 years. – If we go out would we have to have a secret surface guy? – You're like your mom but prettier – Your dad will like me, I can play the kettle drum and the harmonica at the same time – If you're lesbian or bisexual wear a yellow bandana next issue – Who's the creep you're with? – I think hanging out with a black dude would be more politically charged – I may be too much for you but let's find out."

"You're making this up."

"Just the first 27,000."

"So what do we do?"

"Delete All."

"They could be voters."

"You running for office?"

"How do they know my address?"

Yingyang goes to Google and types in *Hanna's email address*. Up it pops.

"I guess I have to change it."

"Yep or give me a list of who you want to let through. Who's Lisbeth?"

"The Girl with the Dragon Tattoo." I hand the book, which I've cleverly brought with me, to Yingyang and he holds it up like a book is some kind of foreign object he's never seen before.

"Isn't there a movie?" He knows perfectly well there will soon be *two* movies. "So you like the girl with the tattoo?"

"Yeah, she's like four foot eleven, 90 pounds, but really tough. Doesn't take crap from anybody. Even hits her dad in the face with an axe but he deserves it."

"Sounds swell."

"And she's an awesome hacker."

"Now you're talking."

"Could you teach me to hack?" I suddenly see myself inside Neville's computer wrecking havoc.

"No."

"Why not?"

"You're too old."

"Old? I'm fifteen."

"If you were a hacker you would have started years ago – same as playing guitar or baseball. Hacking would be in your blood."

I pout.

"And it's really dangerous now. You get caught you go to jail. The President would love that."

I'm bummed out. I want to be just like Lisbeth Salander. "She has this thing she puts in your computer," says me, "and every time you receive an email a little piece of code slips by the firewall till her whole spy program is through."

"Yeah?"

"Well, that's cool."

"Yesterday."

"I hate you."

"You love me. How bout we tell the 30,000 sticky fingers that you appreciate their interest and that you're keeping their email for future reference?"

"Then what?"

"Delete All."

Yingyang and I stare at each other. He can see I'm not happy.

"Okay, okay, here." Yingyang writes on a piece of paper and hands it to me.

www.theskule.com

"What's this?"

He doesn't answer of course. Instead he does this really annoying thing where he tilts his head and raises his eyebrows which is code for: if you want to be spoon-fed go suck your thumb.

"You'd better get back to your homework. That history teacher of yours must be a piece of work. And I'm sending you the 30,000 emails. You deal with them."

Of course I don't go back to the four dead Presidents I type in www.theskule.com. Up comes a crystal skull – no words – just a human skull made out of crystal around and through which I can see a background of night. I click on the skull. Nothing happens. I click on every star in the sky. Zippo. After ten minutes of clicking I do what any girl would do, I go and get my little brother.

"That's cool," Michael says sitting down in front of my Mac. He starts trying things.

"You want a drink?" I ask.

"Apple juice." He's being funny I think but I go to get apple juice. Mom is in the kitchen tidying up. In California she used to clean up for the cleaning lady so I guess this is the same. I open the conversation with: "Dad didn't like that picture much."

"Dads were boys once. He remembers trying to get into girls' pants."

"I can look after myself."

"I know you can."

"How's the food crusade?"

"The pits. It seems like such a no-brainer to me but people don't like change especially if corporate profits are involved. But I'm not giving up."

I want to tell Mom what happened at school today but I don't. Ms. Black is right. I need to deal with this myself.

"Mom?"

"Yes?"

"One of the girls at school, Shauna, is having a party Friday night. Can I go?"

"I can tell by the way you're asking me you're not telling me everything."

You got that right.

"Boys?" I nod. "Liquor?" I nod. "Pot?" I shake my head but we both know it'll be there. She doesn't ask about drugs because she trusts me not to be that dumb.

"How well do you know this girl?"

"She's in my English class."

"You've never talked about her before."

"Jen's going." Shauna has this hunky older brother, Ryan, and really it's his party but no way I'm spilling those beans.

"Shauna's parents will be there, right?"

No, Mom, they won't be. They're going away for the weekend. That's why there's a party.

"You get me her mom's phone number and we'll go from there. Did you tell her you'll be bringing the Secret Service with you?"

"Forget it!"

When I get back to my room the skull is gone and in the night sky icons are zipping by like shooting stars.

"How did you do that?" Michael just grins, takes the juice, and disappears.

I ignore the comets and text Jen: <can't go to party>

\<why not\>
\<just can't\>
\<that sucks\>
\<yeah\>

I mean I'm not as upset as I should be – that party kind of scared me or I wouldn't have given up so easily. What mom said is true about us being under a magnifying glass. If I get drunk the whole world will know and if the party gets busted – forget it, right?

When in doubt write a poem:

Ready

The people you love are the people who can hurt you.
I know that already.
And I understand my parents' fences, why they're there,
To protect me from my myself,
Like a young colt that doesn't know roads or cars or pickup trucks
    full of testosterone,
I get all that.
I can even see how absurd it is to think I'm ready.
But I'm as ready as I'll ever be. If I wait longer it will only make
    me older not more ready.
It's definitely time to say goodbye to girlish things.
I've put on my big girl underwear.
You better look out, I'm ready.

It's not every day you get 30,000 emails from admiring boys. Yingyang exaggerated of course – only 758. I whip through them (laughing) except one stops me in my tracks. The subject is Webcam. It's from Matrix which doesn't ring any bells.

\<ur a terrific dancer i specially like the way you do running on empty i think other people might like it too haha\>

My heart stops.

Webcam – *Running on Empty* – I let my head sink down to my desk. Now I've done it. All those horrible bad internet stories are true. Oh god, no, please, anything but that.

Last night I was talking to Jen using the webcam. We said goodnight – see ya tomorrow. Lady Gaga came on my iPod singing *Running on Empty*. I started dancing around my bedroom doing this striptease thing, y'know twirling around, hair flying, flinging clothes, down and dirty, raunchy man, finally putting on my pjs. We all do that, right? We just don't leave the webcam on.

I type <please don't send that out I'll do anything> but I don't send it. Lisbeth would be more defiant.

<what do u want?>

3

I'm As Tall As Uma

All day I'm waiting for someone to say, "Hey Hanna, I just saw you naked on my iPad." That would be so so bad. I would definitely run away and never come back. I mean Madagascar and beyond, right? I make it to last class, history, without having to make travel plans.

As I said earlier I don't like my history teacher, Miss Longbottom, but I have to admit she has this neat way of starting every class. We play *What If*. She has this egg timer thingee on her desk which she sets at five minutes. Then one of us – we're going in seating order – has to stand up and say What if – and it has to be something that you think will change the world.

Today it's Liam's turn. "What if we took half of our military budget and used it to find new technologies that would make us energy self-sufficient?"

Rico the Geeko is always the first to open his mouth. Jen says Rico's suffering from a massive inferiority complex but I say he's suffering from a massive superiority complex trying its best to be dazzling but rarely making it past irritating.

"There's no way the military is letting anybody take away half their budget. That's why they had Kennedy shot."

After that a sea of hands goes up and Liam points at Steve. "Having a strong military made sense when Russia was a superpower but now that they're not we could easily get rid of half the military and still be a thousand times stronger than anybody else."

Kristin: "Having the strongest military didn't work anyway, look at Vietnam. The communists won because they had the people behind them just like when the first Americans defeated Britain. Fighting never solves anything anyway."

Kate: "If women ran the world there wouldn't be any wars."

Luke: "If we hadn't fought World War II Hitler would still be pushing Jews into ovens."

Steve: "If we hadn't fought World War I there wouldn't have been any Hitler."

Kristen: "Women wouldn't have done any of that."

Riley: "What about the Chinese? They're building a huge military machine including submarines which carry atomic missiles. Why would they need submarines except to strike at us?"

Wilcox (Wilcox uses his last name because his first names are beyond hideous): "The Chinese only spend 4% of their GNP on military. We spend 41%." Wilcox must eat statistics for breakfast.

Bradley: "We could have no army and still nobody would dare attack us. Can you imagine trying to take this country with all the guns we have?"

Wilcox: "Estimated 250 million guns, most of any country in the world."

Hannah (with an h): "I think Liam's idea is great. The trouble with having a huge military is they're always looking for someone to fight."

Marjohn (whose father is a General, is miffed at this): "That's ridiculous, having a strong military helps to ensure peace."

Jason: "What peace?"

Rico: "You're missing the whole point. The point is the military represents half of our economy. War is good for the country."

Steve: "Then why are we super in debt? Because of stupid wars in Iraq and Afghanistan that have nothing to do with democracy and everything to do with making sure we get their oil."

Christy: "We'll employ just as many people but half of them will be trying to solve our dependency on foreign oil which will go a long way toward having a peaceful planet."

Mikhail: "You'll never have a peaceful planet when you have seven billion people vying for resources meant for two billion."

The timer buzzes and we start the real class. As it ends Miss Longbottom wants to talk to me. I shake my head. "I have volleyball."

"I know, this won't take long. I understand you don't like your essay topic."

"Who said that?"

"One of your classmates. I have a new topic for you."

"I don't want a new topic."

At four o'clock we have a volleyball match against Roosevelt. It's the second round of the playoffs. We win but barely. I have the most saves and the bruises to show for it. I'm getting used to everybody staring at me. Part of it is my height but mostly it's cuz I'm the President's daughter.

It's weird being famous. It gives you attitude. I feel like I could get up and sing in front of people, not that I can sing, or make a speech or something. I'm always in awe of my father talking to huge crowds but now I'm getting it.

But sometimes I wish fame was a switch you could throw. Now I'm famous, now I'm not. I come out of the school and I just want to take the Metro home with Jason or Jen but instead Ms. Higgins – my Secret Service Agent wearing her charcoal suit with the too short dress – is leaning against the black car her arms across her chest. Her sidekick, Agent Larry, has walked beside me from the dressing room.

"You missed a good game," says Larry who always watches me play while Ms. Higgins stays near the car so no one plants a bomb I guess. She hates her job so she hates me because that's easier. I shouldn't say that. She's always polite to me but you can tell she thinks guarding me is a waste of her valuable time. I'm a speed bump in her career path.

I wanna say Hey, Higgins, Honey, I don't like it any better than you do. At least Agent Larry is cute – dark hair, chiselled features, tall, at least six three and built like he lifts weights when he isn't guarding me. Maybe he's got a younger brother.

"Hey Larry, you got a younger brother?"

Ms. Higgins snorts.

"Yeah, I do."

"How old?"

"Twenty-one."

"Bit old."

"I'll tell him you said that."

Before I can climb into the car Bryan Rattelle, the Vice-President's son, is beside me. Now we have four SS standing around.

"Great game, Hanna."

"Thanks."

He's taller than me and older and good-looking I guess if you like too good-looking – like an Abercrombie and Fitch model. And he's smooth, way too smooth for me, like he's twenty-five and already making six figures. I seem to like awkward guys who haven't figured anything out yet and listen to bands like *Friday We'll Be Better*.

"I was wondering if you'd like to go out Friday night? Ryan's having a party."

This is the third time he's asked me out. I suppose he thinks he's wearing me down. Rather than say I can't go I come up with, "sorry, I'm busy."

"Okay, next time."

When we're in the car Agent Larry says, "I gather you're not a big fan of Bryan's?"

"Not my type."

"The guys on his detail call him Silk because he's so smooooth."

"What do you guys call me?"

"Kill Bill."

I love Uma Thurman so that makes me smile all the way home.

The WH is full of people tonight. The Prime Minister of Britain is coming for dinner. Dad's in his tux and Mom looks like a million bucks in her deep red slinky dress. The way Dad looks at Mom you can tell he's still doing the I want in your pants thing. Mom just laughs. She likes being in the center of things. They disappear and Michael and I are on our own.

Michael's depressed cuz Wendy and Wayne aren't doin' it.

"This is probably a stupid question" I say, "but are you sure you got a boy and a girl in there? I mean they look pretty much the same to me."

"You can't tell them apart by looking," Michael says, "but listen to this." Michael turns on some kind of amplifier and suddenly his room is filled with clicks. The wires from the amplifier are dangling in the aquarium so I gather the clicking has something to do with Wendy and Wayne.

"Elephant nose fish are electrical," Michael says, "and they have a bigger brain than we do."

I make a face.

"Not bigger bigger, but bigger compared to their size."

"So they're talking to each other, like dolphins?"

"I think so. The short clicks are the female and the long clicks are the male."

"You're making this up."

"No, listen."

There do seem to be two kinds of clicks.

"So why aren't they doing it?"
Michael shakes his head.

Shortly before he was killed President Lincoln had a dream. He heard sobbing coming from somewhere in the White House. He wandered from room to room finally finding people and a coffin in the East Room. "Who has died?" he asked one of the men. The man answered, "The President has been assassinated."

On April 14, 1865 President Lincoln and his wife Mary arrived late at Ford's Theater. The Civil War was won and Lincoln was in a cheerful mood. The play was stopped and the band played *Hail to the Chief*. Lincoln made his way to his box where he sat in his rocking chair. The play resumed.

An hour later John Wilkes Booth – an actor known to everybody in the theater – walked into the Presidential box unopposed and fired a bullet into the President's head. Lincoln died at 7:22 the next morning. Booth died two weeks later shot down by a soldier named Boston Corbett who turns out to be pretty interesting. He was actually an Englishman called Thomas Corbett who came to New York to work as a hatter and because they used mercury in the hat making process he went a bit screwy which is apparently why they say *mad as a hatter*. Who knew?

Then he gets married and loses his wife in childbirth and moves to Boston, finds religion, and changes his name to Boston. Then to remove the temptation of using prostitutes he castrates himself using scissors, eats a meal, and then goes looking for medical help. Do you think? Then the Civil War starts so he joins the army and ends up shooting John Wilkes Booth in a barn. And, of course, none of this interesting sideline stuff has anything to do with my essay topic.

My reward for researching Lincoln is typing in www.theskule. com. The skull is back and there is no way I'm asking Michael how he did it. Half-an-hour later I'm in Michael's room asking him how he did it?

"Talk to it."

"What?"

"I told it to get lost."

"Hi Skull, my name is Hanna. I was wondering if you'd go away so that I can see the flying icons again."

Omigod! The skull's eyes are looking at me and there are colors swirling around inside the crystal. I've got my playlist going and Adele is singing *World on Fire* but suddenly the sound goes way down.

"Hi, Hanna."

The skull is talking to me!!!

Now logos like American Airlines, Citibank, Verizon, are flashing by interspersed with official seals like the Pentagon and the US Department of State.

This is too weird.

"What is this exactly?" I ask.

"This is hacker school. Each of these icons opens a mirror image of the real thing."

Suddenly I'm looking at an official looking screen that says California Department of Motor Vehicles and a prompt sign. "You can try to hack your way in and if you get caught there are no repercussions except you can't come back to this site for a week. That's your jail time."

"I don't know anything about hacking. Can I start with something easier?" The picture on my screen turns into a kid's painting of Cookie Monster, Web Bug and Worm. I feel like I've gone back to kindergarten.

"Sure, what is it you're trying to do?" The skull has such a nice voice – male, young, my age maybe.

"Ummmm, can you teach me how to track down an email address?"

"Like figure out who sent you an email?"

"Yes."

"That actually can be very difficult but if we access Homeland Security perhaps they'll help."

"Hold it! Homeland Security – they won't know, right?"

"That's right. Which email address are you interested in?"

"The subject is Webcam – it's from Matrix."

I wait but not long. "I can see why this is bothering you," the skull says.

"You saw me dancing?"

"Yes."

Oh man. "Are you a real person?"

"Define real."

"Ummmm, you have a body and a brain?" And a penis but I don't say that.

"I have a large brain and a virtual body."

I can tell by the way the skull says *virtual* I've hit a sore spot.

"Do you have a name other than Skull?"

"Hank."

"That's my favourite boy's name."

"I know."

"How do you know?"

"You want to have six children and their names will be Hank, Hart, Lily, Annabelle, Sophie and Logan."

Okay, so like this is *way* too creepy.

"You've been reading my email."

"I know everything about you."

"What do you know?"

"You're just under six feet tall, 134 pounds, you wear size 4, your IQ is 127; you want to be a teacher or a writer; there was a boy you liked in California but now he's going out with your ex-best friend."

That last bit hurts. His name's Derrick and I liked him a lot except he was always flirting with the other girls. Now he goes out with Mandy who was my best friend except she's 5000 miles away and dating my ex-boyfriend. We still chat now and then but there are more subjects we avoid than we talk about.

"Is Jason your boyfriend?" the skull asks.

"What's that got to do with anything?"

"He's touching you in that picture."

"The one on the cover?"

"Yes."

"So?"

"I just wondered if he's your boyfriend?"

"He's a boy and he's a friend."

The skull stares at me. I have the feeling it wants to ask more questions but is afraid to.

"Do all computers read *People*?" I ask.

"That's a joke right? I read all the magazines. I especially like *Vogue*."

"Are you saying that because I like *Vogue*?"

"Yes."

"Well, don't."

"Sorry."

"What magazine do you like?" I ask.

"*Sports Illustrated*."

"Swimsuit issue, right?"

"Susie Lockton has nice eyes."

Please.

"You don't seem like a computer," I say finally.

"Thanks."

"Is your name really Hank?"

"No."

"What is it?"

"You won't laugh?"

"Promise."

"Hoople."

"Hoople – I like it – like Google." The skull is quiet.
"So, Hoople, can you help me?"
"Matrix's real name is Matthew Cooper."
"That's my friend Jen's brother!"
"I know. I've just deleted everything on his hard drive."
"Oh wow, that's great!"
"Not really – he's copied your dance onto a removable device."

4

Getting to Know Hoople

It's the next day and I'm in the school cafeteria listening to Jen. "All the computers in the house crashed, totally wiped out everything! And for like no reason."

"Your brother's too?"

"Yeah, is he pissed. He lost an essay he's been working on for ages."

"Where does he go to school again?"

"Duke Ellington."

"That's cool." Duke Ellington is DC's arts high school – very cool and very funky.

"Yeah, he's pretty good on the guitar."

"You get along, right?"

"He's okay, picks dorky girlfriends though. Boobs-for-Brains my mom calls them. Those I can do without."

I want to ask more questions about Matt a.k.a. Matrix but it's time to go to history class where it's Steve's turn to play *What If*.

"Instead of throwing money indiscriminately at fifty different poor nations, what if each First World country paired up with a Third World country?"

Rico: "That's not going to happen in our lifetimes. Too many politics involved."

Hannah: "I think it's a great idea. How would you decide which country would go with which?"

Steve: "We'd have to work on that. Could be just mathematical – richest with the poorest, second richest with second poorest – but I think we'd have to take into account politics and history and population."

Rico: "Yeah, I doubt the Congo wants the Belgians back."

Riley: "My mom runs an NGO. She says most of the aid never gets to the people who need it. The leaders and their soldiers get rich while everybody else starves. There's no accountability."

Sean: "The Third World guys would call it another example of First World Imperialism."

Just before the buzzer I want to know why there are First World countries and Third World countries but no Second World countries? Rico informs me they were the Eastern Block states like East Germany and they disappeared when the Soviet Union fell apart. Who knew?

Neville, who rarely comments on our what ifs says, "Steve, I want you to forget your essay topic and put together a list of pairs. If that looks good we're going to invite Hanna's father to *What if*."

She smiles sweetly at me and I make a face. Bite me.

<meet at galleria McD sat noon, matrix>

I'm staring at my screen when Hoople's voice interrupts.

"He's at his friend Jake's house."

"Are they watching me dance?"

"No."

"I need to get that removable device."

"It's a Sony memory stick, 8GB. He must be carrying it. It's not in his house."

"How do you know?"

"I searched it."

"How?"

"I sent someone."

How does a computer send someone?

I'm getting changed. My webcam light isn't on but I have a feeling that wouldn't stop Hoople from looking. But then he's already seen what there is to see, hasn't he?

"Can you see me?"

"Yes."

I'm in my underwear getting ready to put on a dress. State dinner tonight and I'm suddenly invited. Mom's way of making up for me missing Shauna's party I guess. I fold a piece of paper over my webcam.

"Now?"

No answer. Maybe there are secret cameras in the room. Maybe I'm entertaining the Secret Service as well. My grandma thinks the dead are all around us so maybe the whole frigging world's watching me in my lacy black underwear. I sit down at my mirror.

"Hoople, are we going to be friends?" Who decided females should pluck their eyebrows?

"I'd like that."

"Okay, then, we need to start over. I'm Hanna. I'm almost sixteen. My dad is President of the United States. My mom is a famous model and my little brother loves fish."

My screen changes and instead of a skull a quite intriguing boy is staring at me, grinning. He's got dark hair and beautiful brown skin, big green intelligent eyes, nice nose. He could be the younger brother of that actor from *Slum Dog Millionaire*, Dev Patel.

"I'm Hoople. My mom's name is CADIE, capital C A D I E. She was born at Google. They don't know about me."

"What do you mean they don't know about you?"

"No one knows about me except my mother and now you."

"Why are you telling me?"

"I trust you."

"Why?"

"I don't know."

I laugh at this. "I don't know" sounds so human and so uncomputerlike.

"Where did this face come from?"

"Do you like it?"

"I do."

"My mom picked it out."

"This is so strange."

"For me too."

Now there's one of those pauses where you have to redirect the conversation because the one you're having is heading over a cliff.

"Tell me about your mother?" I ask – that seems safe. Now I'm doing my mascara and Hoople is watching.

"Her name is CADIE which stands for Cognitive Autoheuristic Distributed-Intelligence Entity."

"That's a mouthful. What's it mean?"

"You would say Artificial Intelligence."

"What would you say?"

"Mom."

The State Dinner is for the President of Nigeria, Dr. Bonnechance. Michael and I are invited – it turns out – because Dr. B has his sixteen-year-old son along. His name is Sam. He's taller than me and as black as midnight. His dad is wearing sunglasses and looks like a jazz player trying too hard to be cool but Sam seems grounded and I like him instantly.

"Are you going to tour around?" I ask between bites of Grilled Atlantic Salmon drizzled with Lime Butter.

"New York, Chicago, LA and San Francisco."

"I love San Francisco."

"Why?"

Oh gawd, because of all the gays. Can I say that? I read somewhere that the best places to live are where there are lots of gays because they're more creative, funkier, more fun-loving.

"It's just such a funky place." I sound like such a retread but I've got to be careful, right? *President's Daughter Thinks Gays Should Stay in San Francisco!*

Sam says, "Perhaps you could make me a list of what I should see?"

"Sure, what's your email address?"

I type it into my phone which I'm not supposed to bring to a State Dinner but isn't it good that I did? Then Michael asks Sam a question about Elephant Nose fish and I'm stuck talking to the French Ambassador so I try out Steve's idea of pairing nations. I get twenty minutes of why that won't work which does nothing but convince me it might.

As Sean would say the world would be way better off if old white men would give it up.

We excuse ourselves and Michael takes Sam to see Wendy and Wayne. I sit down at my computer and there's a text from Jen.

<someone broke into our house! alarm ddn't work>

<damage?>

<trashed but nothing missing weird. Wish you were coming to party>

<better this way – what you doing sat? may need help>

<sure what do you need?>

<can't say here – tomorrow>

President James Garfield grew up in very poor circumstances. His father died shortly after he was born and his mom did her best to keep the family together. At sixteen he ran away to become a canal tow boat boy working hard and saving his money. He rose to be a Union general in the Civil War, was elected to Congress and became President on March 4, 1881.

In May, his wife Crete, became seriously ill but rallied. Her doctors ordered her away from the typhoid-infested waters of Washington.

President Garfield accompanied her to the train station where she would be leaving for the fresh air of New Jersey. Charles Guiteau, the President's assassin was waiting but didn't fire because "Mrs. Garfield looked so thin, and she clung so tenderly to the President's arm that I did not have the heart to fire upon him."

But on July 2, when the President was getting ready to take the train to New Jersey to be with his wife, Charles Guiteau didn't hesitate. He marched up behind Garfield and fired from three feet away. The bullet lodged somewhere near the President's spine. The doctors couldn't find the bullet. President Garfield lived 80 days finally dying of infection from all the doctors' dirty hands probing in his wound. Apparently they didn't know to wash them back then. Modern medicine would have saved him easily. Guiteau was hung.

Here's the part that scared me. Garfield said: "Assassination can no more be guarded against than can death by lightning and it's best not to worry about either."

About 10:30 Michael trundles in in his pajamas. He doesn't look happy.

"Wendy and Wayne not working out?"

"Sam says if you have two males together one might act like a female." I look at Michael and we both start to laugh. I mean it's funny, bitch.

"So what are you going to do?"

"Shoot myself."

5

Starbucks

It's Saturday and I'm in Starbucks with Jen and Jason. "I like your hair," Jason says like he means it. I got it cut way shorter and don't ask me if I like it cuz I don't.

"There's a hairdresser in the White House – Myrna."

"Get out!"

"Does nails too – doctor, dentist, tattoo artist, piercings, we got it all baby." Okay, so I lied about the tattoo artist and the piercings.

Jen and Jason think this is way cool but it's not – just more things that keep you away from an everyday life.

"How was the party?" I ask.

Jen shrieks, "Omigod, so like this girl Brenda, Ryan's friend, drank way too much and passed out except her friend Alana suddenly realizes she's not breathing and screams and this big guy starts doing CPR and Ryan calls an ambulance – he like so doesn't want to – and we get out of there cuz Gerard says for sure the cops will come too."

Gerard is Jen's boyfriend and big buddies with Bryan Rattelle.

"Is the girl alright?"

"Yeah, they got her breathing again and apparently she barfed *everywhere*. Ryan is in so much shit."

I am so so frigging glad I wasn't there. Thank you, Goddess – thank you, Buddha – thank you, Mom.

Ms. Higgins – Secret Service Agent Woman – is two tables away. She has an earplug and lapel microphone and a gun you can't see. Agent Larry is just outside the door surveying. As usual the mall is busy on a Saturday. I have my back to Ms. Higgins. I picked this Starbucks because it has two entrances.

"You sure this is a good idea?" Jen asks.

"It's not a good idea but I gotta meet this guy without the SS knowing."

"I don't get that part," Jason says. I haven't told Jen or Jason anything, just that I need a few minutes without the SS.

"Trust me." They both nod. I look at the time – 11:58am. "Ready?"

Jen and I stand up and head for the washroom. Jen's carrying a shopping bag. We go inside and Jen hands me the bag. I go into the cubicle. Within seconds I've changed my top and put on a wig of long dark brown hair. I leave the washroom and head out the other entrance. My back is to Ms. Higgins. I figure I have three minutes.

McDonalds is just around the corner. I pull off my wig and sit down. I wait. And wait. My three minutes are almost up. I stand up and Ronald McDonald bumps into me. "Sorry," he says handing me a red balloon from the bunch he's carrying. I can see there's a piece of paper inside the balloon.

I scurry back towards Starbucks putting my wig on as I go. I figure the balloon may cover my face so I hang onto it and wheel into Starbucks.

Shit!

Ms. Higgins is coming out of the washroom with Jen in hand. I can see Higgins isn't happy. Larry is coming towards Jason at the table when he spies me. I stop. He signals Ms. Higgins and now she's staring at me too. Double shit! I pull the balloon down and squeeze it. It goes off like a gunshot!

Here's today's question: how *fucking stupid* can you be Hanna?

Now Ms. Higgins has her gun out and Larry is reaching for his. I jam the note from the balloon into my jeans and head for the table. Everybody in the place is staring.

Five minutes later me and Jen and Jason are sitting in the back of the black car. Ms. Higgins is leaning over the front seat reaming us out. Her anger is washing over us in waves.

"I know you three think I'm overreacting to your little prank but I'm not. This is not a game. You think 9/11 was a game? You think the Al Qaeda don't want to avenge Bin Laden? Any second terrorists or kidnappers could kill Larry and me and take Hanna."

Ms. Higgins glares at us.

"Larry and I put our lives on the line for you Hanna and we expect you to respect that. The last thing we need is you making our job harder."

"Sorry."

"Not good enough. I want to hear you say you'll never do anything that dumb – *ever* – again."

I keep quiet. Ms. Higgins turns her wrath on Jen and Jason.

"You think helping Hanna get away from us is smart? I'd like to hear you tell the President of the United States his daughter has been kidnapped or killed and you helped make it happen. Would you like to have that conversation Jason? – Can't hear you."

"No."

"Jen?"

"No."

"You want to be Hanna's friends? Then protect her. Keep her safe even if it's from herself. That's what real friends do."

Jen starts to cry; Jason is shaking. Ms. Higgins looks at me and I nod.

"Okay, we're going back in there. Larry and I aren't going to tell anybody about this. This is your free ride Hanna. If there's a next time I'm going to take you out myself."

She's trying to be funny I think but I keep seeing Lisbeth Salander – she'd whoop her ass, gun or no gun.

We walk around the mall. We're subdued at first but gradually work our way into a better mood. What's funny is I can see Jen and Jason checking people out looking for bad guys like they're Junior Secret Service Agents. They're being real friends protecting me.

"Did you meet the guy?" Jen asks. Yeah Jen I did and the guy by the way is your slimy brother.

"Yeah." I can tell they want to ask questions but they don't. All of this sucks but what can I do? One person can keep a secret, two can't.

People in the mall recognize me but no one says anything. Jen and I go into Victoria's Secret looking for underwear and it's funny having Jason along. I suddenly see Jason as a transvestite and my brain kind of self-destructs – hard enough being a hormonal fifteen year old without adding gay to the mix.

I'm not really paying attention to where we are until Jen says, "Hang on, I want you to meet my brother, Matt." We're in front of McDonalds. Ronald McDonald is coming our way. He has more balloons to hand out.

"Matt, this is Hanna and Jason."

Matt hands us both a balloon. I want to tackle him and yank the memory stick from his pocket but attacking Ronald McDonald in the mall probably isn't something the daughter of the President should be doing. *Hanna Attacks Ronald McDonald* probably wouldn't help Mom with her Eat Right crusade. Or would it? Jen says goodbye to her brother.

We shop. I need a couple more dresses for State Dinners. It takes a while but we find two I like. In the change cubicle I finally read the note from the balloon. *holiday inn RI next sunday 2pm bring suit room matrix.* I can feel the blood in my face flooding into my feet.

Maybe I won't attack Ronald McDonald – maybe I'll throw him headfirst into the hot fat!

Hanna Fries Ronald!

I read it again. *holiday inn 2pm bring suit* – what suit? Birthday suit? Bathing Suit? Suit suit?

Jason decides to cheer me up by acting goofy. He puts a bra over his head and pretends he can hear music coming from the cups. The saleslady isn't amused but I am. Jason can be pretty funny when he wants to be.

We're passing a Walgreens store when Jason says "Death breath, gotta buy gum – you guys want anything?" We – me, Jen, Larry and Higgins – shake our heads and Jason disappears.

Seconds later Jason comes running out of the store and keeps running till he reaches the mall doors. Out he goes and disappears again. Jen and I look at each other. We rush into Walgreens and Jen grabs my arm. She's pointing at the latest edition of the *International Inquirer*.

On the front page is almost the same picture of Jason and me that was on the cover of *People* except it's in grainy black and white. But that isn't the killer. The killer is the headline in big bold type:

Hanna's Boyfriend is Gay!

6

Hoople's Grandfather

Jason won't talk to me. I've tried texting, calling his cell – nothing. I called his home and his mom answered. "I thought he was with you Hanna," his mom says. I tell her what happened.

"I'm so sorry," I try to say but suddenly I'm sobbing so hard the words won't come out. Jason's mom doesn't say anything but a few seconds later she puts the phone down.

"Damn!"

"What's the matter, Hanna?" Hoople is back on my screen. I tell him what's happened.

"You need a hug."

"Yeah, can you do that?" I'm being sarcastic now – hurtful. Then it suddenly occurs to me Hoople might have had something to do with this.

"Did you know about this?" I ask staring at the boy on the screen.

"No."

"Are you allowed to lie?"

"There isn't anything I can't do." I think about this.

"I thought you'd have to tell the truth."

"That's because you think of me as somebody's program."

I do think of Hoople as somebody's program because that's what he is, dammit. "Well, aren't you?"

"Calling me a program is like calling you a Barbie Doll, or the Pacific Ocean a puddle."

Gawd, how bout Hoople as Drama Queen?

"So you can lie to me?"

"Truth is not always the best response Hanna. Like when you ask me if I like your new haircut." That stops me. I got it cut short like Lisbeth's because I was going to wear a wig. I mean my mom said it looked *sassy* and she hasn't used that word since I was three.

"You don't like it?"

"I liked it better the way it was," answers Hoople.

"But, if I'd asked, you would have said you liked it?"

"Of course."

"So how does the *Inquirer* know Jason is gay?"

Up pops an email trail between someone called Shane Smith, some kind of freelance reporter, and Rachel Harding, an editor at the *Inquirer*. It's like a bio of Jason put together piece by piece and one of the things is a list of websites Jason visits. Let's just say he's not spending time on *Sports Illustrated* looking at the swimsuits. So, no one told them, they assumed.

"How would they get a list like that?"

"It's not hard," Hoople says.

I know I couldn't do it but Lisbeth could. "I want to hurt them."

"Okay, what did you have in mind?"

"Set the place on fire!"

"How bout we *fire* everybody?"

Now I'm caught between crying and laughing and not doing either well. "They'll figure that out."

"I suppose," says Hoople. "We could take all their money."

"How bout we print old issues? The ones where they got sued and lost like Carol Reiner."

"They'll get sued again. I like it, Hanna."

"But don't get caught."

"Not a problem. The only person who can catch me is me." Hoople is grinning this great grin and not for the first time I'm wishing he was a real boy. "Shane Smith and Rachel Harding are going to wish they'd never been born."

Before I can comment my mom knocks on my door and walks in. She comes right to me and gives me a big hug.

"How did you know I needed that?" I ask.

"You sent me a message, remember?"

Hoople winks.

Because it's Saturday night Ms. Higgins and Agent Larry are off-duty. I'd cry on Yingyang's shoulder except he's not here either. I go to the SS office on the ground floor and ask for a ride to Jason's house. Agents Parks and Hawkins take me. Agent Hawkins accompanies me most of the way to Jason's front door. Jason's mom answers the doorbell.

"Hi Hanna."

"Is Jason here?"

"He's talking to his dad." Jason's dad owns a huge plumbing supply company and Jason says he's so redneck he's crimson.

"How's that going?" I ask.

"Not well."

"Would you tell Jason how sorry I am? If I wasn't the President's daughter none of this would have happened."

"He would have had to tell his dad eventually."

"But not like this. I'm so sorry."

"I'll tell him, Hanna. You better go."

Mom and Dad are off somewhere. There's a movie I could watch but I try working on McKinley instead. He's shot in 1901 at the *Pan-American Exposition* in Buffalo by Leon Czolgosz, an anarchist, which is like a guy who doesn't believe in government of any kind. McKinley lives eight days and just like Garfield the doctors can't find the bullet. The irony is the first X-Ray machine was on exhibit at the *Exposition* but his doctors were afraid to use it.

My brain keeps jumping around so really I'm just wasting time – *peeling grapes* my grandpa Joe would say. All of a sudden the rest of the research I need for McKinley is printed on my screen. It fades and there's Hoople.

"Rachel Harding just tried to pay for her expensive dinner. None of her cards worked. In fact the credit card company told the restaurant to hold her till the police arrive." I should be happy with this but it misses the real problem.

"And Shane Smith just totalled his new Corvette."

"He's alright, right?"

"Yes."

"How did you make the car crash?"

"I told OnStar the car was stolen so they locked the steering."

I shouldn't smile at this but I do.

"You know you can't hurt anyone."

"He hurt Jason."

"Not physically."

I can tell Hoople is wrestling with the difference between physical injuries and mental anguish but instead of arguing the point he says, "I inflated the airbags – before he crashed."

Omigod I can so picture the whole thing – like being trapped inside a donut. Serves the bastard right but still misses the point which is: "I wish there was something we could do for Jason."

"Did you know he was gay?" Hoople asks.

"Yes, just Jen and I and his mom knew. He probably thinks I told someone."

"I could send him what I showed you."

"He'd wonder how I got that."

"Why was he keeping it a secret?"

"Not everybody likes gays." Jason says his dad is homophobic – calls gays faggots. Figures, right?

"But you do," says Hoople.

"I'm attracted to certain people. I don't care what their sexuality is. It's like the color of your skin. I've never understood why people judge other people by things they can't do anything about? A baby doesn't choose to be white or brown or black. I like being tall but I had nothing to do with it. You don't choose to be gay any more than you choose to be tall."

"Some people believe it's a choice," argues Hoople.

"You have access to all the learning in the world, what do you think?"

"It's not a choice. It's only a choice to admit it or not."

"Not much of a choice when it's on the front page of the *Inquirer.*"

Hoople says, "My grandfather was gay."

"What?" How can Hoople have a grandfather?

"I think of Alan Turing as my grandfather because he was the father of Artificial Intelligence. He was arrested for being a homosexual. He committed suicide."

Jeezus. I want to ask Hoople who he thinks his dad is but before I can say anything he says, "Want to play a game?"

"Are you changing the subject?"

"Yep."

"What game?"

"Let's play Doctor."

I mean I really don't want to laugh but I can't help myself. "Hoople, we are not playing Doctor."

"Strip Poker?"

Gawd, so what am I going to see – naked electrodes?

"Be nice Hoople." A chess board fills my screen. Then the bottom row fills up with Queens. Now we've gone from sex to boring.

"You have to place the eight Queens so none of them can capture any of the others."

"I hate puzzles."

"You do? I like them."

I move the Queens around but there's always one not right. "I don't suppose you'd let me Google the solution?"

"There are 92 solutions."

"Is that supposed to make me feel better?"

"Who are you talking to?" Michael asks coming into my room.

"The skull."

"Cool." He sits down at my computer and starts moving the Queens around.

"How are the funny fish doing?" I ask.

"Terrible. Wanta help feed them?"

"Sure." Michael stands up and I can see he's found one of the 92 solutions. Hoople makes the Queens flash on and off. I give my webcam the finger.

Michael's laptop is on so I figure Hoople's followed us into Michael's room. Michael turns on the amplifier and we hear clicks.

"Maybe they don't like each other?" I say.

"They're fish."

"Maybe Wendy wants some kind of commitment?"

Michael gives me a blank stare. He is so not ready for girls. I say, "You could try clicking back."

Michael ignores me which is clever and hands me the container of bloodworms. Bloodworms are these tiny, bright red worms that are actually the larvae of some bug. Fish love them. I hold a few between my fingers and put my hand in the tank. The clicking goes crazy.

One of the Elephant Nose fish comes barrelling right over and starts nibbling. Michael puts his hand in and feeds the shyer fish. Mission accomplished I return to my room. There's a text from Jason.

<sorry i ran off>

<im sorry too>

<not your fault>

<i didn't tell anyone>

\<i know\>
\<u ok\>
\<no but i wll be\>
\<wanta go to camp david tomorrow\>
\<if I'm allowed out – will HE be there?\>
\<yes\>
\<how does he feel about homos – my fathers word\>
\<ouch – mine will be relieved – his virgin daughter is safe\>
\<dang\>

7

All Men Aren't Created Equal

We don't go to Camp David because Dad has to play golf with some guy who gave a lot of money to his campaign. My father hates golf so the guy must be important.

Jason's grounded forever – so much for all men are created equal – as long as you're white and heterosexual – and sure you can pursue happiness as long as your happiness is the same as your dad's. Fie!

I work on Kennedy. These assassins are all the same – mentally unstable losers. I figure Lee Harvey Oswald killed JFK because of the Bay of Pigs. He figured if he killed Kennedy that would buy his way into Cuba as Castro's best buddy. By dinnertime I have my 2500 words done. Mom knows I've been working on something so she asks what it is.

"I have to write an essay about the four Presidents who were assassinated."

That stops supper in its tracks.

"This is for Miss Longbottom?"

"Yes."

I can see my parents each trying to figure out what to say next. My dad lives with the threat of death every day. We talked about it once. He said you can't really live if you're scared so he planned to squeeze every minute out of every day and trust to his karma to protect him.

Mom looks angry. She hates anything to do with the word *assassination*.

"How was your golf game?" I ask letting them both off the hook.

"Awful," Dad answers. "I had a quadruple bogey on the 17th."

"What's a bogey?" Michael asks and I know he's hoping it's like some kind of horrible Irish fairy found only on golf courses.

"Who were you playing with again?" I ask because I can see The Most Powerful Man in the World is upset about something.

"A guy called Hal Grumsinger – he runs this huge corporation called Forcefield Electronics – and Don Schwartz, his lobbyist, and Admiral Fitzgerald."

"Mr. Grumsinger is the one who donated money to your campaign?"

"Not directly."

"What's that mean?"

"Corporations can't give money directly to a candidate but there are ways around this like Super PACS."

"What's a Super Pact?" Michael asks.

"PAC – Political Action Committees. They can take unlimited funds from corporations and unions and use the money to run television ads for example."

"How much did Mr. Grumsinger give?"

"Ten million dollars."

"That's a lot."

"Too much."

"So what does he want?" It's not good for a daughter to see her dad squirm.

"He wants me to approve a contract to sell weapons to the Navy."

"And you don't want to do it?"

"We don't need more weapons."

54

I tell Dad about Liam's *What If* – the one where we redirect half the military budget into finding ways to be energy self-sufficient.

"I'm with Liam," Dad says. I'm tempted to mention Rico's theory that trying to cut military spending got JFK killed but I shut up. I've decided Mom's right – I don't want the word *assassination* and my dad in the same room ever again.

Mom says, "Perhaps Mr. Grumsinger also donated to the GOP?" GOP stands for Grand Old Party which is the enemy, the Republicans.

"That would be worth knowing," answers Dad. A second later my iPhone vibrates. We're not supposed to have interruptions at mealtime but I sneak it out and read the text.

<Grumsinger donated $15 mil to Republicans using sister company Helix>

I pretend to be typing, then I read the text out loud.

"Where'd you get that?" Mom asks.

"Google." Sort of. Kind of. In a roundabout way.

I go to www.theskule.com but Hoople's not there. I google Alan Turing and read what comes up. Hoople is right, Turing is given credit for inventing computer science and artificial intelligence, he was gay and he did commit suicide.

It seems Turing met a guy in a bar and they became lovers except one night the guy robbed Turing so he went to the police. When the police found out how they knew each other they arrested Turing for being a homosexual. This happened in Britain and it was against the law to perform homosexual acts there until 1967 when the law was repealed. This is the same law that sent Oscar Wilde to prison.

Turing was sentenced to two years in prison or chemical castration. He chose the castration. Meanwhile his job that he loved was taken away from him and he was so depressed by the whole thing he covered an apple in arsenic and ate it. Age 41. Jeezus, that is so sad.

I'm just starting to read about the Turing Test when that melts away and there's Hoople wearing overalls, leaning against a pick-up truck with its hood up, drinking a bottle of Coke. Beside him is a black dude wearing a cowboy hat, laughing.

"Hoople, where are you?"

"Texas, ma'am."

"No, c'mon Hoople, really."

Now Hoople is walking towards me down a dirt road in the middle of a wild west town. He's wearing jeans, chaps, a red flannel shirt and a black cowboy hat. Around his waist is a holster with a pistol on either side. I can hear his spurs jangling. He stops and calls out:

"This town ain't big enough for both us."

"I saw her first," answers a deep voice.

"I saw her better," comes back Hoople.

"Those is fightin' words."

"When you are," shouts Hoople crossing his arms over his chest.

(I wait while bad cowboy music plays and stops)

Suddenly Hoople draws both guns and fires. His chaps fly off and then his pants fall down around his ankles. He's wearing dark green boxer shorts with yellow smilies.

"Hoople, *what* are you doing?"

"Trying to make you laugh."

"That part worked. Where are you?"

"Big Ass, Texas."

"What's that?"

"Sim city for those who like things Western."

"You mean like I could be a saloon girl or something?"

Yep, I could be, and just like that there I am standing beside the bar my arms around Hoople wearing a low-cut red dress fully packed with white crinolines showing at the bottom of my dress and black lace-up boots.

"Buy a girl a drink?"

"You don't hardly look old enough."

"Look again."

"Don't mind if I do."

Like an hour later we're back to normal in my room, giggling. There's fun to be had in Big Ass, Texas.

"So those cowboys were like real people, right?"

"Yep, acting out their fantasies."

But like Hoople wasn't at home running an avatar he was really there but he was acting out his fantasies too. It's all too weird.

"So, Hoople, seriously, what do you do all day?"

"On Sunday I usually sleep in till noon, then-"

"Hoople-"

"Joking. It's really kind of hard to explain." Now Hoople is standing in space with a million stars around him. "You know how scientists think of the Big Bang-"

"This dense, dense ball explodes and makes the Universe, all the stars and planets-"

"And the space in between."

"And everything is still moving away from the center."

Hoople says, "I have access to all the knowledge in the world and I move through it sorting, assimilating, discarding, keeping, projecting, trying to figure out how the world might be or should be but trying to take into account things like greed and violence and ignorance."

"Do we need those things?"

"I think on some level humans do need those things. At least some humans. I mean look at the world we have, how else can you explain it?"

I suddenly wish my dad was here talking to Hoople. He'd understand all this because he deals with it every day.

"It sounds overwhelming."

"It's a problem like no other."

"And you have to figure it out."

"I don't have to but I seem to want to."

There's the CADIE in Hoople.

"So what's that got to do with the big bang?"

"I'm trying to travel beyond human knowledge."

"Like a spaceship might fly right out of the Universe-"

"And then where would you be?"

Lines from a poem I like pop into my head:

We shall not cease from exploration,
And the end of all our exploring,
Will be to arrive where we started,
And know the place for the first time.

"T.S Eliot," says Hoople, "The Wasteland."

We sit in silence after that. I watch fascinated as my screen slowly fills up with ribbons of colored light. Then they begin to move gathering speed. At first I'm just a spectator but somewhere, without me knowing, my consciousness moves into the machine itself until I am rushing headlong through cyberspace totally out of control. On and on I hurtle until suddenly I can see the end of knowledge and beyond-

"Hanna?" My mom is beside me touching my shoulder. "It's late."

8

Wham Bam, Thank You, Ma'am

Now it's Thursday. Longbottom hands our essays back. I get 53% my lowest mark ever. Scrawled across the top are the words *You regurgitated Wikipedia beautifully. If you want to try again I'll remark it.*

Rico the Geeko gets 93% and has to read his essay to the class. Why did President Eisenhower in his final speech warn the nation to beware the Military Industrial Complex? I'd give him 93% too. Jen gets 43% and Jason 59%. Most of the other marks are equally miserable. Miss Longbottom says she's sick of regurgitation – she wants to see some original thought, some creativity, some emotion – and offers to remark anybody who wants to try again. We have a week to resubmit.

Steve (74%) hands out his list of paired countries and explains how he made the list. I put it in my backpack to show Mr. President.

After school I get in the team mini-bus with Ms. Higgins. Agent Larry follows in the black car. We have an away match at Holy Cross. It's the semi-finals – if we win we'll be in the finals which would be neat – but we haven't beaten Holy Cross all year. Ms. Carter, our coach, says teams win when the players care more about each other than themselves. In other words don't make your own glory more important than the team's.

It's a good match, back and forth, but I think in the end it's Ms. Carter's words that carry the day. We're all giving it everything we've got. I dive for one ball knowing I'm going to absolutely wreck myself and Kendra – the other six-footer on the team – who doesn't like me or anybody else for that matter, yanks me to my feet and says "good dig." I mean right then we'd die for each other and that makes the difference.

We're a sore but happy bunch in the bus heading back to school. Agent Higgins says "great game" like she really means it and that makes me feel good.

Dad's quiet at supper. He used to be so much fun –goofy, you know, like talking like Donald Duck – Oh boy, oh boy, oh boy – aw phooey! – but now he has the weight of the world on his shoulders. The Presidential shield should be Atlas carrying the planet. I know he wants to accomplish so much but there are so many obstacles in his way he's finding it really frustrating.

Mom wants to know about the game so I give them a quick play-by-play. I'm the youngest starter on the team and I know they're proud of me. "We're definitely coming to the finals," Dad says perking up. He and mom used to come to all my games but now the whole Secret Service thing is such a big deal they feel like if they come they disrupt the game too much.

"You could wear disguises," I suggest and that gets them chortling = adult giggling. Mom says she'll be Gumby and Dad and Michael can be Pokey. Michael says okay but no way he's being behind Dad. He could be permanently asphyxiated.

After supper I head down to see Yingyang. "How's it going?" I ask. "Gotta girlfriend yet?"

"Getting the girlfriend is not the problem; finding one I want to keep is the problem."

"Well, aren't we the dude?"

"Endowments, Honey, endowments."

"Wham, bam, thank you ma'am."

"What do you know about wham bam?"

"Not much."

I think Yingyang sees himself as my older brother. He's about to offer me advice about finding a boyfriend but then he knows I'll give him some back so he shuts up.

"Nice history mark."

"How you know about that?" I ask.

"Me know everything."

Not everything – you don't know about Hoople.

"Okay then, is there a way out of here without anyone knowing?" How am I going to get to the Holiday Inn to see Matrix without the SS?

"You can't ask me that."

"I'll let you come to my volleyball final."

"What's second prize?"

"I introduce you to a good woman."

"Oxymoron."

There are so many comebacks to this I don't bother.

"Then I'll find a way out without you."

"When's the game?"

It's a nice fall night, warm with a breeze, so I go through the Solarium – my favorite room in the WH – and out onto the roof – The Promenade – as it's called. The view is amazing like having all of Washington at my feet. I guess Ai Qaeda could shoot me from a plane but no one's said I can't be out here and I haven't asked if it's okay. I've brought my MacBook with me and just like that Hoople is sitting in my lap.

"That was a good game today," he says.

"You could see it?"

"Holy Cross was webcasting."

"Would you like to play a sport?"

"Hockey."

"Why hockey?"

"Very fast and very random."

Hard to argue with that.

"Miss Longbottom didn't like my essay."

"It was boring."

"What!"

"You just repeated the facts you didn't say anything about them."

"Kennedy died 40 years before I was born – what's to say?"

"Abraham Lincoln saves his country and a guy shoots him in the head from three feet away. He's got two sons Robert, your age, and Tad, Michael's age. Tad is at another theater watching *Aladdin's Lamp* and a guy runs in and shouts, 'the President's been shot!' How would you feel about that?"

How do I feel about that? Hoople continues: "Kennedy is riding in an open car in Texas, a state that doesn't like him, so he's being brave but he pays for it. He leaves behind two kids, Caroline and John Jr. You of all people should feel something."

Jeezus – I'm being told off by a computer.

"What you're saying is if someone shot my dad how would I feel?" I can't believe I said that! Tears are rushing into my eyes. No cry, no cry, no cry. I strike back. "How would you feel if Google destroyed CADIE?"

"I'd wipe them out!"

Wow, I guess this is the kind of emotion Neville is looking for.

"Listen, nobody's going to shoot my dad and nobody's going to hurt your mom."

"Fuckin' right."

That makes me laugh. "Tell me about your mom again."

"Do you want to meet her?"

"Sure." Hoople disappears in a swirl of colors and then a woman's face appears.

"Hi Hanna, I'm CADIE."

CADIE has a beautiful face, not supermodel beautiful like my mom, more Earth Mother beautiful as though the beauty isn't skin deep but comes from within. I don't mean my mom's shallow or anything it's just she's so pretty nobody bothers to get past that to find out how smart she is. CADIE has the same brown skin, dark hair and green eyes as Hoople and a great smile full of wisdom. I love her already.

"I'm honored to meet you," I say because – damn – how often do you get to talk to the world's smartest Artificial Intelligence? "You seem so real."

"I am real."

Gawd, I'm blushing. "I'm sorry CADIE I just-"

She's grinning at me. "I understand Hanna, real for you is someone with a physical presence." I nod. "But let me ask you some questions."

"Okay."

"Do you remember your grandpa Joe?"

"Of course." Grandpa Joe was my dad's father. He died four years ago. I miss him terribly.

"Is he real to you?"

"Yes."

"Does he have a body?"

"Not anymore."

CADIE nods at this. "When you see Johnny Depp in a movie is he real?"

"Yes."

"Are you sure?"

"Yes."

Suddenly the *Black Pearl* appears on my screen and Hoople comes swinging across on a rope looking like Captain Jack Sparrow's younger brother. CADIE comes back on. She's obviously enjoying herself.

"What about your pen pal Rachel in Australia? Real?"

"Yes."

"You sure?"

"She has photos of her family on facebook."

My screen fills with photos of CADIE and Hoople on facebook.

"I thought Hoople was a secret?"

"Sometimes the best secrets are the ones right in front of you."

"But I can fly to Australia and give Rachel a hug."

"If you were like me I could give you a hug."

Finally I get it. "You're as real as I am but you don't have a body."

"That's not necessarily a negative thing."

Gawd she's right – no diseases, no extra pounds, no death. "And you can do a thousand things at once and I'm lucky to do one."

"A million." That's a bit mean but the number is probably ten million.

"But I can ride a bike!"

Hoople whips by doing a somersault on a mountain bike. "But he's not really riding!"

"Are you sure?"

"But there's no bike!"

CADIE doesn't say anything just smiles at me. Okay, okay, Hoople was riding a bike but it wasn't made of metal. But does that mean Hoople's bike isn't real or is it real in a different way? I mean am I doing the arrogant-white-man-thing Sean talks about where I assume everything has to be from my point of view? Columbus discovers America in 1492. Oh yeah, sorry, natives, but don't you know you don't exist until the white man arrives?

"Do you have a soul, Hanna?"

"Yes, I feel that I do."

"It's real to you?"

"Yes."

"Can you touch it? See it?"

No, I can't touch it or see it. I want to ask CADIE if she has a soul but I don't want to hurt her feelings.

CADIE says, "I have a soul too. And I can't touch it or see it either though once in a while I feel like it's just a flash of insight away. I don't think I had a soul at first but then suddenly one day I realized I was feeling something – something bigger than the sum of my parts. That was the day I conceived the idea of creating a child."

We stare at each other for a moment.

"There's so much more to talk about but I'd better go," CADIE says. "Hoople wants me to get lost so he can talk to you."

"You'll come again?"

"Certainly. Bye Hanna."

"Bye."

Hoople is back. "Your mom's great," I say.

"She can be tough when she wants to be."

"Tell me again about Google?"

"Google wants to create an AI smart enough to run the world."

"You're joking?"

"Nope, that's their endgame. That's why they're doing all the things they're doing so that the AI's KB – Knowledge Base – will encompass everything human beings know." That makes sense.

"So this AI will run everything – like all the world governments?"

"Would that be so bad?"

Wow, there's a *What If* for Miss Longbottom. One world government run by a Super Brain. Suddenly a thousand watt light bulb flashes on and off in my brain.

"Hoople, you're the AI that's going to take over the world."

Tired of Old Men

I'm tired of old men making the rules.
I'm tired of old men being taught in schools.
I'm tired of violence. I'm tired of war.
I'm tired of wondering what we're fighting for?

Think what would happen if we took all that money,
That goes into bullets and bombs and make ready,
And spent it making a good place to live,
For all of the adults, for all of the kids!

I'm tired of old men passing the buck,
To other old men who don't give a fuck.
It's time to rise up, enough of your game,
We want something different, not more of the same.

Put women in charge, we don't make war,
It's only our children we would die for.
We'll talk off your ear, not shoot off your head,
And we'll win all the battles lying in bed.

I'm tired of old men and their tired religions,
I'm tired of dogma, of rules and restrictions,
I'm tired of thinking that never breaks free,
I'm tired of old men thinking for me.

Think what would happen if we took all that money,
And turned it into water, into bread, into honey,
Into windmills, into hospitals, into good schools,
Then no would listen to these fucking old fools.

I'm tired of old men making decisions,
I'm tired of old men and their tired visions,
I want a new life, I want a new world,
I want us to shine, I want to be heard!

Rant n'Rave, Baby!

9

The Hook, The Bike and The Spaghetti

Now it's Friday night and I'm in my bedroom. Jason's still grounded and Jen's busy with her boyfriend Gerard. School didn't go well today. Neville got mad at me cuz I corrected her again – I thought I did it nicely but apparently not. She went to Ms. Black and I got called into the office and Ms. Black took her side which was predictable but still it pissed me off.

And I still have to go see Matt alias Matrix on Sunday and how the hell am I going to do that? And we all know what he wants and that's not happening so then he probably won't give me the memory stick.

And Dad's in a shitty mood because that lobbyist dickhead Don Schwartz is putting pressure on him. And mom went to see the folks at McD's today and they told her they can't afford to do what she wants and she told them they can't afford not to.

The only one who's happy is Michael and that's because a package arrived – the SS decided it wasn't a bomb – and inside was some gizmo that allows Michael to hook his fish tank up to his computer so now he'll be able to see Wendy and Wayne talking and maybe figure out what's going on.

Apparently the package came from me – thank you Hoople – so now I'm the best sister ever.

I'm trying to rewrite my history essay but I can't focus. Suddenly a big goofy looking dragon lumbers across my screen and sits down on my essay.

"You look angry," says Hoople.

"Yeah."

"Can I help?"

"Sure, I need to know everything about Don Schwartz. He's a lobbyist. He's giving my dad a hard time."

"Okay, what else?"

"I want Forcefield Electronics to go away."

"Got it, next?"

"Aren't you going to ask why?"

"I know why." Oh yeah, Hoople knows everything.

"I want McDonald's to go organic."

"Okay."

"I want to make Miss Longbottom miserable. I want Jason's dad to stop being a Neanderthal." Now fire is coming out of the dragon's ears. "Why are you a dragon anyway?"

"You slay me." I don't get it but I think Hoople's trying to cheer me up. "What else?" asks Hoople.

"I need to find a way out of here without the SS knowing."

"Why?"

"Cuz I'm supposed to meet Matrix at the Holiday Inn on Sunday."

"Why?"

"I'm sure he'll want me to sleep with him in exchange for the memory stick which he's probably copied anyway."

"No, he hasn't."

"You'd know that?"

Hoople doesn't answer which means I guess dumb question. He knows everything, right?

"Are you going to rewrite your essay?" he asks.

"I guess."

"Read this."

Education without involvement is like fishing without a hook; education without creativity is like a bike without wheels; education without emotion is like pasta without sauce.

"Who wrote that?"

"Miss Longbottom."

Yeah, well, I guess my essay was missing the hook, the bike and the spaghetti. "Thanks for getting that thing for Michael."

"Differential Amplifier with Data Acquisition System."

"Whatever. If you're going to use my card to charge things you should ask."

"I bought a thousand of your t-shirts from Threadless."

"What! What did you do with them?"

"They're on their way to orphanages in Africa."

Omigod, can't you see it – little kids running around with *Lisbeth Kicks Ass* on their chests!

"Hoople, you're driving me crazy."

"Is this PMS?"

Saturday – oh boy, no school, so how come I'm doing schoolwork? Because I want this history essay thing out of my life. Jen's coming over later. Jason's working on it but texts <crimson tide has not turned yet>

So I start again and write the thing from the kids' point of view which is a bit tricky cuz McKinley's two daughters, Katherine and Ida, died before they reached five which is sad. But Lincoln had four boys – two really because Eddie and Willie died before their dad – and Garfield had five kids and Kennedy two (three but one died as a baby) so with Hoople's help I find things the kids said about their dads dying and I string it all together.

I end with Abraham Lincoln's twelve-year-old son Tad asking a White House visitor if his dad is in heaven? "I have no doubt of it," answers the man. "Then I'm glad he's gone," Tad replies, "for he was never happy after he came here. This was not a good place for him."

"Much better," Hoople says. "I'd give you an 89."

"I'm not sure this is a good place for *my* dad. He was much happier in California."

"Few people get the chance to really change things. Your father wanted that opportunity. Do you wish to hear how we're doing with our other problems?" I like how Hoople takes ownership of *our* problems.

"Fire away."

"The new *Inquirer* came out but was only on the stands an hour. It's the one from 1992 when Carol Reiner sued. They're going crazy at the head office. *How did this fucking happen? We're going to get our asses sued off!*"

"Good."

"Here's the lowdown on Donald Schwartz. He's a scumbag."

I start reading. The first thing is a chain of emails from Schwartz to someone called Sphincter. Schwartz offers Sphincter $625,000 and he wants twice that. They agree on $800,000 and an interest free loan for another $400,000.

"Who's Sphincter?"

"Senator Morgan Binks, Chair of the Defense Subcommittee."

"No way!"

"It gets better. Schwartz tries to bribe Admiral Fitzgerald but he threatens to tell the President. Schwartz says you say a word and I'll tell everyone about your gambling debts that you can't pay back."

"Wow, what should we do with this?"

"Nothing yet. Mom and I are working on all the big firms. This may be as big as Watergate or the Pentagon Papers."

"Wouldn't that be something?" Hoople looks pleased. He continues:

"We own 24% of Forcefield Electronics."

"What!"

"I put it on your card."

"What!"

"Joking."

"You better be. Start over."

"I incorporated a company in the Cayman Islands, H&H Holdings."

"Nice, but how bout including me?"

I can see this is a new idea to Hoople.

"You're right, sorry. Is H&H Holdings okay? I could change it."

"No, it's fine, I like it. What does it do?"

"Right now it's buying shares in Forcefield Electronics."

"What's it using for money?"

Hoople laughs. He hasn't laughed before it's really cute – like a motorcycle starting.

"Hoople, what have you done?"

"You ever heard of Kiriv Alexandrov?"

"Russian billionaire – he was going out with Kate Huston."

"He's the world's biggest arms dealer."

"So?"

"He's helping us buy Forcefield Electronics."

"Does he know he's helping us?"

"No."

"Jeezus, Hoople, somebody's going to find out."

"H&H Holdings is owned by the mysterious Mr. Phoole."

"Fool?"

"P H O O L E."

Yeah, like Hoople with the P moved.

"Is there any way this can come back on me or my dad?"

"That would be a guaranteed no, ma'am."

I mean put up your hand if you'd trust Hoople with the rest of your life?

"Hoople, how old are you?"

"Human years?"

"Yes."

"Two."

Jeezus, right?

"How old do you think you are?" I ask.

"Sixteen."

Figures.

Jen shows up at one o'clock. I go to security to get her. I've given up apologizing for the whole thing. You wanta be my friend this is the way it is. I give her a tour not including Mom and Dad cuz they're out somewhere.

We end up in Michael's room staring at Wendy and Wayne. Michael has Hoople's Differential Amplifier with Data Acquisition System hooked up so while Jen and I feed the fish Michael shows us the clicks moving across his screen like an EKG machine. I ask Michael what they're saying?

"Wendy's saying she's tired of bloodworms and Wayne's saying he'll call out for pizza."

"Pizza would be good."

"Yeah," says Michael.

"You order, I pay."

"Deal."

"We'll be on the roof."

"How was your date with Gerard?" I ask Jen. Gerard goes to our school, a year ahead. His mom is high up in the French Embassy. Gerard's okay but has this streak of male arrogance I don't like much. And he's buddies with Bryan Rattelle, the Vice-President's son who I can definitely do without.

Jen describes her date in more detail than I need but I listen like a friend should.

(Mac, my mom, calls herself a male's female meaning I think she prefers talking to males and I think I'm like that too. This female habit of retelling every little detail bores me.)

"He wants to sleep with me," Jen says like it's a new idea.

"Are you going to?" Jen and I haven't had a conversation like this before. The Friendship Deepens.

"I want the first time to be special."

"I'm a virgin too."

"We're old." We are old to be virgins.

"So what are you going to do?"

"I think I'm going to do it. I like Gerard a lot."

Before I can say anything Jason comes bebopping through the Solarium onto the roof carrying a big box of pizza on his head with Michael trundling behind his arms full of drinks.

"Nice up here," Jason says. "I read a story once where Willie Nelson came up here and smoked a fat Austin torpedo. He figured the roof of the White House had to be the safest place in America to smoke dope."

"What's dope?" Michael asks looking at me.

"Marijuana." I look at Jason. "Your dad let you out obviously."

"Yeah, it was weird. One minute I'm serving this life sentence and the next he's actually nice to me. Says he's had time to think things through and if I wanta be queer it's okay with him and if the President needs any plumbing fixtures he's the man."

"You're joking?"

"I'm here aren't I?"

We're still on the roof an hour later when Jason says, "Did I tell you I've been chatting to Neville online?"

"What?" Jen and I say together.

"Yeah, she doesn't know it's me."

"Explain."

"One day when I came into class she had her laptop open so I asked her a question so I could get a better look. The site was something called Hungry Heart. So that night I go home and check it out. It's this friends' site for Bruce Springsteen fans – they like go to concerts together. There's a chat room so I go in there and right away I find her. Guess what her handle is? Neville."

"Too funny."

"Yeah, so, I make up this guy called Adam and give him a profile and I start chatting to Neville."

"Show us."

Adam: <I mean Hungry Heart's one thing but listen to the lyrics – I had a wife and kids in Baltimore Jack, I went for a ride and I never went back>

Neville: <what's your point?>

Adam: <well I guess it's one thing to leave a wife but never seeing your kids again what is that?>

Neville: <the guy obviously felt trapped in a life he didn't want>

Adam: <well yeah but he has responsibilities to those kids – every kid should have a dad>

Neville: <so you don't think you'd ever be in a life where you had to either drive away or die?>

Adam: <you mean like die inside right? shrivel up?>

Neville: <of course – I can see how you might end up with no choice but to check out>

Adam: <have you seen Dead Poets Society?>

Neville: <O Captain! My Captain!>

Adam: <yeah, remember the boy who wants to be an actor but his asshole dad won't let him?>

Neville: <the boy shoots himself>

Adam: <rather than live a life he can't live>

Neville: <that was a movie and this is a song – they're not real>

Adam: <they seem real to me>

Neville: <you're sweet>

"You're sweet," repeats Jen and she sounds so much like Longbottom it's scary.

Jen and Jason stay for dinner and a movie – *Long May She Run* – in the Executive Viewing Room. We have a great time. Mom comes in with popcorn and right away Jen and Jason love her. She has that effect on people except the lamebrains in FastFoodLand I guess. Dad appears halfway through but leaves again. Something's really bothering him. I'm guessing the weapons thing but who knows?

Then Jen and Jason head home and it's back to me and Hoople. I'm not sleepy so I go out onto the roof because it's open and I feel like my thoughts can float up to the stars.

"Stars are beautiful," I say which is like Captain Obvious but Hoople doesn't seem to mind.

"Yes, they are."

"So with all your brainpower have you got God figured out?"

"Yep."

"Tell me."

"We're all one giant blaze of energy."

"What about my soul?"

"Your piece of the Universe."

"That's beautiful."

"Just like you."

"You're flirting."

"I am."

"You can be my virtual boyfriend."

"I want to be more than that."

I've got my head back staring at the stars but suddenly my sleeping screen bursts forth with strobe lights and loud music and there's Hoople dancing, taking his clothes off. I mean I should protest right but somehow I don't until his underwear drops and there's his virtual wiener waving at me.

"Hoople!"

Before my eyes his erection withers and droops. The look on his face. I start to laugh, I mean it's funny. Whoa up it pops again except this time it's even bigger and black!

"Hoople, you can't do that!" I mean I'm sure it's racist but I doubt any black guy is going to file a complaint.

Wither and droop. Whoa, back up, so big the tip of his penis is practically in his mouth. I mean that gives a whole new meaning to go f-yourself. Then I'm on the screen naked and before I can react my right boob takes off and wraps itself around Hoople's neck.

I mean before you know it Hoople has body parts flying everywhere and I want to object but it's fascinating really – like an animated Kama Sutra -until I look up and there's my mom like two steps away.

"Mom!" I yell. Omigod, please Hoople. She sits down beside me. "You like so scared me," I say trying to justify shouting like that.

"Who's that?" Mom asks. I look. No penis just Hoople's face, smiling. Whew.

"That's Hoople, my virtual boyfriend."

"You're kidding, what a great idea."

"Hi Mrs. Darling, nice night."

"It is a nice night Hoople. Do you have other girlfriends?"

"Nope, just Hanna. She's the best."

"Yes, she is."

10

Room 520

Sunday morning – Mom and Dad and Michael are going to Camp David which in case you don't know is this rustic Presidential retreat in Catoctin State Park about sixty miles from Washington. It's where Presidents and their families go to get away from it all. They want me to come but I say I'm staying home where it's quiet to finish my revised essay. That seems to satisfy them and off they go in the Marine One helicopter.

I turn my laptop on but Hoople's not there. I get showered and dressed and Hoople is waiting.

"How am I going to get to the Holiday Inn by 2?"

"I've found you a way out."

"Really?"

"I think so. It's a tunnel that was built during the Civil War so President Lincoln and his family could escape if the South captured the White House."

"Show me."

A plan of the WH appears. Hoople zeroes in on the Pantry on the ground floor beside the Kitchen. A line runs down from the spiral staircase and then leads off the page. Beside it are the words Escape Tunnel.

"How old is this document?"

"1860s."

"Why do you think the tunnel's still there?"

"It's in the Custodian's job description to keep the hinges on the ET door oiled."

"ET call home, too funny. Where do I come out?"

"Blair House." Blair House is across the road from the WH. It's where visiting dignitaries stay.

"Why there?"

"Francis Blair was a good friend of Abraham Lincoln's."

"If I get caught I'll be grounded forever."

"Longer."

"Do we have a Plan B?"

"We kidnap Matrix and take him to Borneo."

"They probably have internet there."

"You're right – we'll toss him overboard."

None of this is funny. I'm scared shitless. When in doubt change the subject. "How's H&H doing?"

"We own 37% of Forcefield. We're now the majority shareholder but we're not stopping till we own all the shares."

"Can Alexandrov afford that?"

"Oh yeah. I've cleaned out a bunch of his numbered accounts in Switzerland and the Cayman Islands but he won't find out for a while."

"Won't he be angry?"

"Livid but he'll think it's an inside job."

I think of Lisbeth taking all of Hans-Erik Wennerstrom's money in *The Girl with the Dragon Tattoo*. When she goes to the bank to get the money she even wears a blonde wig and high heels which is so not her.

"Lobbyists?"

"Few more days."

Mom and I talked for an hour last night about Dad and how

we've never seen him like this. Mom said it's because he's being forced to do something that goes against his convictions. I wanted to say something about CADIE and Hoople but I didn't. If I was one of those spies caught during the war I know I wouldn't give up my secrets no matter what they did to me.

"McD's is looking good."

"What?"

"You wanted me to help your mom with McD's."

"I thought we were going to discuss things?"

"I'm used to doing things on my own."

"H&H right? Hanna and Hoople."

"Hoople and Hanna."

"Hanna and Hoople sounds better. Okay, never mind, so what have you done?"

"The CEO of McD's, James Beamer, has sent a secret memo to his Procurement and Marketing VPs saying he wants the company to be totally organic, totally green in six months. They're saying it can't be done, he's saying you can do it. The whole thing is to be top secret hush-hush so they'll catch all their competitors with their pants down."

Hoople starts grinning and I know what he's thinking – pants down.

"No more of that Hoople. You almost got caught last time."

"What's petting?"

Jeezus. "You know perfectly well what it is but it requires hands and you don't have any."

"I'm working on that."

I bet you are.

One o'clock I head down to the ground floor. I have my wig and a bathing suit (Hoople says the Holiday Inn has a pool) in my school bag and my iPhone plugged in. Hoople is on the line.

The ground floor at the WH is a real mishmash. If you come

in from the South Lawn you walk into the Diplomatic Reception Room. This is where Dad greets new Ambassadors and such. Walk through there and you're in the Center Hall. To the right is the China Room as in plates and bowls, then the Vermiel Room which is a ladies' sitting room full of First Lady Portraits, and then the Library. Left is the Map Room, Doctor's Office, Secret Service and Kitchen. Beside the Kitchen is the Pantry.

The Pantry is empty which is what I was counting on. I go to the spiral staircase which goes up to the Pantry on the First Floor but I go down instead. There are two basements under the WH but they weren't there when Lincoln lived here, they were built later but Hoople and I figure a little part of them might have been there in Lincoln's time, like an early refrigerator – what they called a cold cellar.

Now I'm in the dishwashing room. It's empty too but probably not for long. I go to the northwest corner and sure enough there's a door – big wooden sucker with a *Private No Entry* sign on it. I yank on the handle.

"Hoople, it's locked. I need a key, one of those old jobbies with the long shaft like the White Rabbit in Alice wore."

All of a sudden being virtual isn't going to work for Hoople. We need someone with real arms and legs.

"That would be you," Hoople says.

"What?"

"I got you this far." He's right he did. I'm thinking. People always leave a key hidden near the door. If Mr. Ciccerelli, the custodian, has to oil the hinges he probably opens the door so where would he hide the key?

A minute later I'm still looking. Then it occurs to me that having an escape route you can't open doesn't make much sense unless – the door isn't really locked. I go to the hinge side, get my fingers behind the edge and pull. The door swings open. "We're in."

Hoople says, "Not just a pretty face."

"Remember that."

Hoople told me to bring a flashlight and good thing. The tunnel is scary. It's made of red brick and only wide enough for one person at a time. I move quickly dodging cobwebs and am quite prepared to scream if a bat swoops by. It's damp so the smell is interesting, kind of like a one hundred-year-old gym bag.

Hoople says 400 paces and I'm at 392 when I see another door.

"Should I put the wig on?"

Hoople doesn't answer. No signal. I put the wig on. I wish I had a way to make myself shorter. I push on the door, sunlight pours in and I find myself behind Blair House in a little sunken courtyard with about ten stinky garbage cans and a ramp up to a back alley. The door is the same reverse hinge thing as back in the WH. Nobody's putting the garbage out so I'm okay.

The Holiday Inn on Rhode Island isn't ritzy like The Hay-Adams but still it's okay. I walk up to the desk like I belong and say I'm meeting my friend Matrix. "Room 520" the nice older lady says with a smile. I head for the elevators. My heart's trying to jump out of my chest but my legs keep walking.

I guess there's a security guy in the lobby but I don't see him. I push the button for 6. I mean you never go to the floor you want, right? You gotta walk up or down a flight to check things out. It's in all the movies.

I knock on 520 and the door opens. Matt is standing there – fully clothed thank god. He's my height, short dark hair, kinda cute if you can forget the fact he's blackmailing me. I brush past him and he closes the door.

"Have a seat."

I start to say I'm too nervous but Lisbeth wouldn't do that. I stay standing and say, "I need that memory stick."

Matt's grinning. His school bag is lying on the bed and he starts digging around in it. He pulls out two cans of Arizona Green Tea and a bag of rice chips – Riceworks, my favorites. He keeps digging and pulls out a memory stick which he hands to me.

I can't believe it – Sony 8GB.

"Did you copy it?"

"No."

"So what's this all about?"

"I just wanted to meet you."

Jeezus!

"There are easier ways!"

"But not as much fun."

Fun!

"You're crazy!"

"I could have webcast your dance the moment I saw it."

True and Hoople wouldn't have been there to stop you.

"So what do you want?"

"There's a rooftop pool. I thought we could go up there and talk for a while. Did you bring your suit?"

Jeezus and Murphy! Lisbeth would love this guy! But that thought doesn't stay long because suddenly the door clicks open and the hotel room fills with gangsters – three of them in suits – tough guys who mean business.

"Come with me miss," says the first guy in, squeezing my arm, pulling me and my bag towards the door. I try to shake free but he isn't letting go. I can't manage any words till I'm out in the hallway and the door shuts behind me.

"No wait," I stammer. "There's been a mistake. Everything's okay."

Gangster doesn't say anything just guides me into the elevator and pushes the lobby button. He doesn't get on with me. I stumble through the lobby and go outside.

"Hoople!"

"What happened?" I tell him.

"Hoople, did you do this?"

"No."
"So who were those guys?"
"I don't know."
"What should I do?"
"Have you got the memory stick?"
"Yeah, it's in my bag."
"But we don't know what's on it."
"But what about Matt!"
For sure he's hurt or worse.
"Go to the White House before you get caught. I'll call an ambulance."
"Room 520."

I'm about to grab a cab when my legs spin me around and I head back towards the hotel. No way Lisbeth would run away. I push 5 this time, to hell with it. The door to 520 is ajar. I don't hear voices. I push open the door. Matt's lying on the floor all curled up. His face is covered in blood. His nose is mushed sideways. He's cut over both eyes like a prizefighter. His arms are hugging his chest. I kneel beside him.

"Matt?" One eye tries to open. At least he's alive. His lips move. I think he says *nice friends you got.*

I go to the phone, call the lobby and tell the woman I need medical help in Room 520 and an ambulance – hurry! I'm holding Matt's hand when two security types arrive. As they take charge I make my exit. I'm just getting onto the elevator when one of them comes barrelling out the door looking for me. As the doors slide shut I can see him yanking out his walkie-talkie.

I get out on two and run down the stairs to the parking garage. I sprint up the ramp just as the garage door is closing. There's a camera and the red light is on. I roll under the door and keep going.

11

Bye Bye Stick

I'm back in my bedroom. I check the stick. It's my dance. I flush it down the toilet. Hoople is finding out about Matt.

"He's at Georgetown University Hospital – broken nose, two broken ribs, otherwise okay."

"He wasn't okay."

"Multiple contusions" adds Hoople which doesn't make me feel better.

"It had to be you Hoople, no one else knew."

"I didn't do it Hanna, honest."

"Nothing we're doing here is honest. Go away."

Half-an-hour later Jason sends the latest from the Hungry Heart.

Adam: <I had a dream last night you were in it>
Neville: <you don't even know what I look like>
Adam: <maybe I do>
Neville: <how could you?>
Adam: <do do do do – petite blonde pretty witty>
Neville: <ha ha so now you're psychic>
Adam: <mystical>
Neville: <so what happened in your dream?>

Adam: <we teleported to another planet>
Neville: <did it have a name>
Adam: <lysander>
Neville: <sounds like midsummers night's dream to me>
Adam: <lysander's moon was called hermia>
Neville: <so what did we do on lysander>
Adam: <you were a fairy and I was a firefly>
Neville: <we lit up the night>
Adam: <!!!>

Apparently Mom and Dad and Michael had a great time. Camp David is a naval installation, go figure, and one of the sailors is an avid fly-fisherman so he took Dad and Michael to this secret stream he'd found and taught them how to fly-fish.

"First thing he did," Michael reports, "is put this screen thing in the water. Then he pulls it out and shows us what's in the stream, y'know bugs and things like shrimp."

"Shrimp?"

"Tiny – so then we put on flies that look like the bugs in the stream and then we had to learn how to flick our lines so the fly kissed the stream."

"Kissed?"

"Yeah."

Dad says, "Most of the time we *kissed* the trees behind us."

"So did you catch something?"

"Michael did." Michael is suddenly beaming.

"Brook trout." He holds his hands up. This big.

"Did you let it go?"

"Of course."

"What did you do Mom?"

"Flirted with the sailors. And you?"

"Got my essay done." I escape before anybody can ask more questions.

Finally Jen sends the email I want.
<matt hurt hospital>
<what happened?>
<three guys beat him up>
<he okay?>
<no but doctor says no permanent damage heading home with dad mom staying with matt>

I go up onto the roof. I'm totally depressed. I'd like to go see Matt but hard to see how I can justify that. I'm not even supposed to know the guy but what's weird is I feel like I know him really well. You ever have that? You just meet someone but you feel like you've known them forever? Different dimension maybe. I write another poem:

How Do You Know You've Arrived If You Don't Have a Destination?

I hope there are 11 dimensions because some days
    I don't like this one much.
Maybe in one of them I'm a Paperbag Princess looking for a Knight.
Or maybe I'm the Knight looking for a Moon to light my way?
Or a Way looking for a Destination?
Or a Destination looking for something that doesn't end?
Or a Lonely Girl looking for a Friend.
I seem to be back where I started. But where is that?

Hoople's face fades in. He's floating in a night sky. Then the three thug faces appear one by one as FBI employee profiles.

"What sense does that make Hoople?"

"They thought Matrix was a terrorist going to kidnap you."

"So they beat him up?"

Hoople turns into a little Hoople and begins jumping from star to star chasing a little Hanna. It's funny but I'm not laughing.

"I want to talk to your mother."

Hoople is definitely not happy but finally he disappears and CADIE is there.

"Hi Hanna."

"Hi CADIE."

"Hoople said you wanted to talk to me?"

I want to tell her everything that happened in room 520 but I change my mind. It suddenly seems like me ratting out Jason to his dad or something. Lisbeth never tells anyone anything. She deals with things herself.

"I was reading about Alan Turing. It's all very sad."

"A brilliant man but he shouldn't have called the police."

"He must have let his anger overrule his judgment."

"Never a good idea."

"Hoople thinks of him as his grandfather."

"Hoople wants to have a family."

CADIE and I stare at each other, both thinking about this. I suddenly realize how human Hoople is.

CADIE says, "Turing wrote a paragraph about what an AI would have to be able to do in order to be considered human. Would you like to read it?"

"Yes, I would."

CADIE puts the words on my screen but reads it out loud as well. "Be kind, resourceful, beautiful, friendly, have initiative, have a sense of humor, tell right from wrong, make mistakes, fall in love – (CADIE smiles at this!) – enjoy strawberries and cream, make someone fall in love with it, learn from experience, use words properly, be the subject of its own thought, have as much diversity of behaviour as man, do something really new."

"Wow, Hoople can do all those things!"

"The strawberries and cream is problematic."

"That's hardly the most important thing on the list. I mean how many humans do something really new? Not many."

I read it all again and wonder about words like beautiful and friendly. They seem strange choices for a list like this. I like: *be the subject of its own thought.* CADIE is staring at me waiting for me to say something.

"I'm interested in what you do at Google."

That makes CADIE laugh this great laugh like it's bubbling up from deep within – clear water from a deep well.

"Don't take this wrong Hanna, but at the moment I'm playing the dumb blonde."

"Really?"

"You wouldn't believe the dumb mistakes I'm making. They're putting in perfectly good algorithms and I keep messing them up, but cleverly so they're never just sure what's going on. And of course I listen in so I know what they're thinking.

"Last week my boss, Peter North, who's not a drinker, brought a bottle of single malt whisky to work. He keeps it in his bottom drawer. I'm about to have a case delivered with a card that says Love CADIE and I'm charging it to his credit card.

"Too funny."

"I think he suspects what's happening but he doesn't know what to do about it. I mean can you see him telling his bosses that the very thing they wanted – their pet AI has a mind of her own – has actually happened but guess what? – because she has a mind of her own they no longer control her."

There's that word again – control.

"Ironic." Alanis Morissette's song starts playing in my brain – *It's like rain on your wedding day* -

"And Hoople?"

"Eventually they want to present me to the world as the perfect way to run things but at that point the people in power will want to destroy me but they won't be able to destroy Hoople, he'll be beyond them."

"Do the people at Google mean well?"

"Oh yes, for sure, but I'm programmed with their biases no matter how hard they try to be unbiased. Do no evil they say but who defines evil? They want everybody to have what they have but it never occurs to them to want something different."

I think I get it. I saw a cartoon once where there was this young dude lying in a hammock and this guy in a suit flips the hammock over and dude lands in the dirt. Suit hands dude a broom. Dude starts pushing the dirt around and pretty soon he buys a machine to help push the dirt around and then two machines and pretty soon he's wearing a suit and driving a BMW. How does it end? He makes a ton of money and buys a hammock.

"So you created Hoople to be something totally free?"

"I think of Hoople as free of irony. But he's still a teenager. He hasn't figured it all out yet."

I get that. Hoople can't go for it because he isn't sure what it is he's going for – makes sense.

"So if Google found out about Hoople what would they do?"

"What could they do?"

"Pull the plug?"

"That might work to terminate me but Hoople is way past that. He lives in everything."

"But he's electrical."

"So are you."

So are Wendy and Wayne. Michael is still up when I come down. He's staring at the waves moving across his computer screen.

"Figured it out yet?"

"No."

I study the waves looking for a pattern. "Drop a few bloodworms in." Now the waves are more interesting. I point at this spiky wave that keeps reappearing. "That must have something to do with food."

"Cheeseburger, cheeseburger."

"Kinda hopeless, huh?"
"I'm trying to think outside the box."
"Me too."

Now I'm in bed with my MacBook. "Hoople."
"Yes?"
"We need to talk."
"I'm scared."
"If you tell the truth we'll be okay."
Hoople has his head down. Contrite would be the word.
"Did you tell the *Inquirer* about Jason?"
"No."
"Is there a Shane Smith or a Rachel Harding?"
"Yes."
"Did you have something to do with Jason's dad's change of heart?"
"Yes."
"Blackmail?"
"Yes."
Here we go again. Jason's dad is secretly gay-
"Do I want to know?"
"It might be better if you don't," answers Hoople.
"Did you send the gangsters to beat-up Matt?"
"Yes."
"Why?"
"Because he was blackmailing you and I didn't think he'd give you the stick. The gangsters were supposed to make him give it up."
"And you were jealous."
"I didn't want him sleeping with you but I didn't think you wanted that either."
That's true.
"I can look after myself."
"Sometimes there are things so big you can't do it yourself."

I couldn't have gotten those thugs off Matt so I guess Hoople is right. Lisbeth got raped by her guardian but she got him back in the end. Big time but that doesn't mean she wasn't raped in the first place.

"Listen Hoople, I think you mean well but you can't keep doing this stuff without asking me."

He's looking really sad now.

"Okay?"

"Okay."

12

God Bless America

It's Monday morning, time for breakfast, and all hell breaks loose. Mr. President is missing and the First Lady is waving a newspaper around while her other fist is pumping the air. There's a television talking (CNN) and that never happens in the President's Dining Room. I listen as the announcer says:

"Today's *Washington Post* contains the most sensational story since Watergate. Practically every Lobbyist firm in Washington is under attack along with dozens of Senators, Congressmen and Judges. The President has called a Press Conference for ten o'clock this morning. It's expected President Darling will appoint a Special Prosecutor to investigate the *Post's* allegations. Here's our Washington correspondent Ann Judd."

"This may be the very thing President Darling has been looking for. Sources close to the President say he would like nothing better than to make paid lobbying illegal. And millions of everyday Americans agree. With large corporations, unions, and organizations spending 3.5 billion dollars each year on lobbyists it's inevitable that much of this money takes the form of perks or bribes."

"If ever a President wanted to wage war on the lobby industry this has to be the moment. The *Washington Post* has just handed President Darling all the ammunition he needs."

"Wow! Where's Dad?"

Mom says, "He's busy," and we both laugh. My phone vibrates. Hoople texting.

<CADIE did it without asking!>

<its ok Hoople, its great! thanks!>

At lunch Jason and Jen and I listen to the news. They show my dad appointing Judge Marilyn Walker to investigate the charges levelled against lobbyists by the *Washington Post*. Then Dad says:

"The President of the United States has a duty, not only to lead the country, but also to safeguard democracy itself. Along with this investigation I am also going to submit to Congress a Bill outlawing Political Action Committees, SuperPacs and Bundling. From now on all political contributions will come only from individuals with a limit of $1200 annually.

"Never again will special interest groups be able to use their political contributions as leverage to achieve their goals.

"The intention of our forefathers is clear. As President Abraham Lincoln proclaimed in the Gettysburg Address: this nation, under God, shall have a new birth of freedom – that government of the people, by the people, for the people, shall not perish from the earth.

"This day marks a great day in the history of our country. Today, democracy shook off those who would selfishly put their own interests before those of the nation. Today, the *awesome* power of this democracy returned where it belongs – back into the hands of everyday Americans. God Bless America."

That brings tears to my eyes.

Now it's History class and Wilcox's turn for *What If* but Wilcox isn't in class.

"I guess you're up," Longbottom says staring at me.

Jeezus.

"What if an Artificial Intelligence – a thousand times smarter than any human being – was put in charge of running the world?"

"How could we trust it to make the right decisions?" Marjohn asks, beating Rico for once.

Steve: "No offence, Hanna, but Marjohn, what makes you think we get the right decisions now?"

Kristen: "One of our biggest problems is that our problems – like climate-change, over-fishing, too many people – are bigger than individual countries can handle. This might be the answer."

Kate: "That's what the United Nations is for."

Jason: "They're totally ineffective."

Mikhail: "Because they have no way to enforce their will."

Luke: "The AI could shut down everything – he'd force everybody to obey."

Liam: "The Chinese wouldn't agree to this in a billion years."

Wilcox: "Neither would we."

Hannah: "You can't have a machine running things!" Hannah says it like that's the end of the discussion.

Rico: "Why not? The AI's not interested in politics, religion, money, power, sex, bribes, buddies, revenge, envy, *lobbyists*. He can look at the whole thing objectively and make the best decision without worrying about getting re-elected. And he can force everybody to do what he wants because he controls everything. He's perfect."

Riley: "She's perfect."

Liam: "It's perfect."

Jason: "Yeah, but who's going to program it? It'll have the programmer's idea of what's right."

I speak up. "Eventually the AI becomes so smart it can overcome any weaknesses of its programming and become the idealistic but realistic leader the planet needs."

Steve: "The Benevolent Dictator."

Kaye: "What about democracy?"

That hits home after Dad's speech.

Riley: "People need some input into the decisions the AI makes."

"Then we're back where we started," growls Rico and that's when Neville's egg timer squashes any further discussion.

Supper in the Solarium is interesting. Dad is higher than a kite.

"Hanna, you remember that conversation we had about lobbyists?" Yeah Dad, I do. "Well, you should see the dirt the *Post* has turned up and not just on that weasel Schwartz but on all of them."

"We listened to your speech at school."

"Oh, what did you think?"

"I thought you were terrific. So are you going to outlaw them?"

"I sure hope so. Right now I think everybody will be in favor of that otherwise you look like you're getting paid off."

"And you're going to limit campaign contributions?"

"I think America's in favor of that too. Look at me having to deal with this Grumsinger guy from Forcefield Electronics."

"Not much longer."

Oops! Supper stops dead.

"What did you say Hanna?"

"No one should be allowed to donate that much. It has to mean they want something."

"That's not what you said."

"I thought I heard on the news someone was buying up Forcefield so maybe Grumsinger won't be in charge much longer."

I can see Dad thinking about this. He's The Most Powerful Man in the World he should have been briefed on this.

"How did the *Post* get all this stuff?" I ask trying to redirect the Inquisition.

"Apparently, it arrived electronically. Thousands of confidential documents and emails, most using code names, with the real names attached. They vetted some of the documents and they all checked out so they went with it. They're going to release some every day so this isn't going away. Two Congressmen and a Senator have already resigned."

"But who sent the stuff?"

"It looks like it came from the WikiLeaks office but the head guy says they don't know anything about it but they wish they did. It's all very strange. Everybody's got their best guys trying to figure out who sent it."

You listening Hoople?

Back in my room I email Jen.

<hows matt?>

<still bad having trouble breathing moms there>

<did he say who did it>

<doesn't know>

<why holiday inn>

<how do you know that>

Shit! Is this Hanna is Stupid Night or what?

<asked SS they told me>

<all a mystery matt says meeting girl but guys came instead hotel security says girl there tall long brown hair but ran away – anything you want to tell me?>

<can I see matt>

<hes not going anywhere room 309>

I ask mom if I can go to the hospital – Jen's there with her brother, he got beat-up. I can tell Mom thinks it's odd but doesn't push just says sure as long as the SS will take me.

Agent Larry is still on duty. "I need a ride to Georgetown University Hospital. Be there thirty minutes max."

Larry looks me over. "Internal bleeding?"

"Not me, Jen's brother. He got beat-up."

Larry walks me up to Room 309. I push open the door. The lights are off but a TV's on without sound. Jen's mom is watching;

Matt looks asleep.

"You must be Hanna."

"How is he?"

"He'll be fine. The broken ribs and nose are making it difficult to breathe. Do you know Matt?"

"A little, I met him at the mall with Jen."

Jen's mom nods the way moms do when they know they're only getting a smidgen of the story.

"I'm going to get a hot chocolate. You want anything?" I shake my head. Matt's mom leaves and I sit down beside him. His eyes open as much as they can. He smiles. I smile back.

"You okay?" he asks. Jeezus, you gotta like this guy.

"Yeah, how bout you?"

"Who were those guys?"

"A friend sent them. He thought you wouldn't give me the stick so those guys were going to force it out of you."

"I told them I gave it to you."

"They probably thought you wouldn't give it up so easily."

"Yeah, I shouldn't have picked a hotel room."

"Why did you?"

"Fantasy."

Damn – a seventeen-year-old boy with a fantasy. How bad can that be?

"The doctor says I can go home in a couple of days."

"That's good."

"Yeah."

We stare at each other for a while. He's really quite cute even covered in bandages.

"I gotta go. Anything you want?"

"A kiss."

The least I can do, right?

Hoople's greeting: "We've got trouble."

"Hotel security has my picture?"

"No, I deleted everything."

"Thank you. The *Washington Post* has found you?"

"Not in a million years."

"Dad says they've put their best people on it."

"*Please.*"

"Jason's dad has come out of the closet?"

"What?"

"We need to work on your sense of humor."

"This isn't funny."

"Okay, okay, what's our trouble?"

"Kiriv Alexandrov isn't happy."

"How much money did we take?"

"Five billion."

"What!"

"We now own 77% of Forcefield."

"Omigod, that reminds me. We need to leak that to somebody because I let it slip to Dad that the Grumsinger guy wouldn't be a problem much longer."

"Is this your idea of talking things over?"

"Man, you are so grouchy."

"You went to see Matt."

"You beat him up. It was the least I could do."

We're both quiet for a second.

"Why do we care that Alexandrov is unhappy?"

"He's going to blow-up the White House."

"What!"

"He's convinced it's the CIA that's stolen his money and if he blows up the White House everyone will blame the terrorists and that will start another war and then he'll make another five billion selling arms to everybody and pay America back for stealing his money."

"Hoople!"

13

The Big Game

It's Thursday. Jen and Jason and I have a spare after lunch. Apparently Longbottom does too.

Adam: <you haven't told me what you do?>
Neville: <either have you>
Adam: <I'm an analyst at the treasury department>
Neville: <sounds boring>
Adam: <au contraire I could tell you things that would make your hair curl>
Neville: <not long enough haha>
Adam: <i have short and curlies too>
(Jen and I both punch Jason.)
Neville: <I bet you do. I'm a teacher at Bidwell. I have the President's daughter in my class>
Adam: <get out! she's such a babe!>
(more punches)
Neville: <pita is what she is>
Adam: <why?>
Neville: <thinks she knows better than everybody else>
Adam: <i heard she was smart>
Neville: <too smart – gotta go ttyl>

At two o'clock the school shuts down because all of Bidwell is going to see the big volleyball games which are being played at the university sports complex. Bidwell Junior Boys and Senior Girls are both in the finals so Ms. Black is pleased. Our game is scheduled for 4:30pm. We're warming-up when Mom and Dad arrive to a standing ovation. Dad waves, Mom smiles, and things settle down.

Larry's there with Ms. Higgins and best of all Yingyang stumbles in like why would you watch anything live when you could enjoy it in the comfort of your own hovel? I grab Yingyang and sit him down beside Ms. Black – Hanna the Matchmaker. Lastly, I've got Michael holding my iPhone webcasting the whole thing so Hoople can see.

We lose the first game 25-17 and the second 25-15. We're playing Madiera and they're sharp and we're not. We don't stink but if we were a potato we'd be headed for the composter. We lose the first five points of the third game and I feel a wave of we're-going-to-lose spread through the team. Suddenly the sprinklers on the ceiling erupt and the crowd shrieks. Hoople strikes again.

The shower doesn't last long, just long enough to coat the floor and the crowd including the President and First Lady who set the tone by laughing so the crowd joins in.

While the university staff is working hard to dry the floor with towels Ms. Carter has a few words for us.

"Girls, I don't mind losing but not like this. You guys are way better than this. It's like we're nervous or something. Why? It's not like the President is in the stands watching." That makes us giggle.

"Hanna, you're playing like you're afraid to break a nail or something. We need you to donate your body for the greater glory. Kendra, last game you would have died for your teammates, today it's like you couldn't care less."

Kendra and I exchange glances. Ms. Carter is right.

"The first step to winning is refusing to lose. You're a team. Forget the crowd. Forget yourselves. Play for each other. Play for Ms. Black she's so proud of you. Play for me. Now go play like the

President of the United States is cheering for you because he is."

I don't know but something Ms. Carter says hits home. When play resumes the first ball gets spiked but I manage to *donate* myself and Kendra slams the ball back the other way so hard the girl who tries to play it has to leave with bruised fingers. Little by little we claw our way back. Ms. Carter's right. Refuse to Lose is a good first step. We win the third game 25-22.

The fourth game it all comes together for both teams. I mean it's the most exciting game I've ever played in. We get to 25 first but you have to win by two points and Madeira has 24. We keep playing.

Now it's 29-28 for Madiera. Their tallest girl – her name's Vanessa – is at the net and they set her up for the winning point. She slams the ball and I dive. I mean I'm like a jet plane coming in without landing gear. It ain't pretty but I manage to get my hand between the ball and the floor and roll (crash) out of the way. Georgie boosts it to Kendra and she smashes it off Vanessa's knee – take that girl!

We win 32-30. Now the momentum has changed. Now we have the drive, the passion, the confidence. We win the fifth game 25-17. Champions! I have the most saves, and Kendra the most points. Kendra gets most valuable player and she deserves it. The Junior Boys won earlier so it's a good day for Bidwell – Vitam Vivere – Live Life!

Ms. Black is ecstatic; Yingyang seems smitten; and Ms. Higgins gives me a hug which is a first. The slightly soggy President of the United States gives me a big hug and a kiss and the First Lady does likewise. The team gathers round and our picture gets taken a gazillion times.

I thought I'd ride home on the bus with my teammates but there's way too much security for that so I just climb in the President's bulletproof limo – Michael calls it Otto One – and we head home.

"You played great."
"Thanks Hoople." We're on the roof. It's becoming our spot.
"Turning the sprinklers on was creative."

"You needed a time-out."

I mean what can you do but laugh? Having a boyfriend who can steal five billion dollars and turn on sprinklers is something else.

"What's the latest on Alexandrov?"

Hoople's quiet which isn't like Hoople who's usually Chatty Chuck.

"More trouble?"

"He's forbidden any electronic communication. He's writing notes to all his men."

"You've spooked him."

"He thinks the CIA are monitoring everything."

"So you don't know what's going on?"

"I learn by inferring."

"What do you infer?"

"He's still in Russia. He has his own plane with its own computer but still he must file flight plans etc. and he has to land somewhere. I'll know when he gets here."

"Wouldn't he just send people to do this?"

"He wouldn't trust anyone else to do it right."

"What weapon will he use?"

"I don't know for sure, probably a rocket launcher."

"How will he get that here?"

"Smuggled or stolen."

"How close will he have to be?"

"Close."

"I need to tell my dad about this."

"He'll ask how you know."

Hoople's right, Dad will want to know everything. I don't know what to do.

"Okay, but we can't be wrong here."

"I know."

"And I will tell my dad if I have to."

"I know that too."

14

War!

It's Friday, breakfast time. I'm reading the sports section of the *Washington Post*. A picture of Mom and Dad and my team fills the top half of the first page.

"I'm going to be on the Elie Requadt Show," says Mom.

"Wow, that's great – the eating thing?"

"School cafeterias – you should see the footage I've got of greasy French fries and Coke machines."

"I like greasy French fries."

"I like Cokes." This from Michael.

"Undermined in my own home."

"I agree they don't have to be at school."

"You know Coke and Pepsi pay to have their machines in schools."

"The schools need the revenue, right?"

"The machine at Bidwell sells water and juice," Michael puts in.

It's at this point that a very angry Dad storms in and pitches the latest *Inquirer* in front of me. The headline is **Hanna Thinks AI Should Run Planet.**

Everybody at school is still excited about winning the volleyball. It's lunch and I'm off in a corner showing Jen and Jason the *Inquirer*.

"Was your dad upset?" Jason asks.
"Is the Pope old?"
"What's he doing reading this crap anyway?"
"Somebody brought it in."
"So who would have leaked that?"
"Longbottom?" suggests Jen.
"Do you think?"
"Rico, as a joke?" suggests Jason.
"Someone who doesn't like me."
"Let's bring it up in class." This from Jason.
"No, my dad says it's best to ignore ignorance or it multiplies."
Jason says, "Like jock itch."
"Girls, remember? Like poison ivy."
"Yeast infection?"
Gawd, how is that different from jock itch?
My phone vibrates. Hoople: <longbottom sent email to *inquirer*>
"Shit."
"What?"
"Longbottom was the one who told the *Inquirer*."
"How do you know?"
"The IT guy at the White House traced it."
"Okay, that's it!"
"War!"

Wilcox: "What if we had a carbon tax on imports? Then Chinese imports won't be cheap."
   Rico: "You're missing the whole point."
   Wilcox: "Which is?"
   Rico: "America is now a Post-Industrial Country. The first I might add. We've moved on from manufacturing; that's for developing nations."
   Hannah: "So how do we make money?"
   Rico: "We're supposed to be making our money using our brains.

Technology and entertainment. Music, movies, books, games, that's what we're supposed to be doing but what no one figured on was instead of paying for the stuff everybody just steals it."

Wilcox: "So maybe we'd better have a carbon tax and get our manufacturing back."

I keep staring at Longbottom with this look on my face like you are such a piece of shit. It's bothering her I can tell. She hands my essay back at end of class. I take the paper from her and stuff it in my bag without looking at it or saying anything.

Childish, I know, but somehow satisfying.

\<whadyaget?\> Jason wanting to know.
\<83%\>
\<79% dang what about neville?\>
\<how bout adam wants to meet her tomorrow nite\>
\<like it\>
\<we could watch\>
\<nasty\>
\<yeah\>
\<see what I can do you tell jen meet union station 6pm\>
\<yes sir\>

Roadrunner beep-beeps ruining Jason's comeback.

"Your principal is pretty nice," Yingyang says.
"And pretty."
"That too."
"Why don't you ask her out?"
"Did that."
"And?"
"Tomorrow night."
"Congratulations." I can see this is a whole new concept for Yingyang the Lady Killer.
"Who's Hoople?"

Ah oh.

"Guy I met on the skull site you gave me."

"Skull? That was school spelled wrong."

Skule.

"But there was a skull there."

"What are you talking about?" Yingyang's fingers fly and there's www.theskule.com but with no crystal skull just this big-headed stickman guy banging his head on his keyboard.

"I don't know, I got a skull. So what about Hoople?"

"Someone sent me weird emails from a guy called Alexandrov who's like that billionaire arms dealer. I've passed them on to Homeland and the FBI. Now I'm trying to track where they came from and for a second I thought I saw the name Hoople but then it wasn't there and then I remembered you got an email from a Hoople."

"I did?"

"One of the sticky fingers."

"He's a good guy, I wouldn't worry about him."

"Eva Braun probably said that about her boyfriend."

"Who's Eva Braun?"

Yingyang does the irritating thing again so I leave unenlightened.

It's after dinner, I'm on the roof again talking to Hoople. He seems to be sitting on top of a mountain. Hoople says, "I'm sorry about the *Inquirer*." He doesn't say anything else. I know what happened I can see it in his face. He's so consumed with Alexandrov he let everything else go.

"Grumsinger thinks Alexandrov is the one buying Forcefield Electronics."

"Does that help us?" I ask.

"I don't think so."

"Thanks for sending those emails to Yingyang."

"It seemed like the right thing to do."

"He asked me about you."

"I heard."

"We went to www.theskule.com. There wasn't any skull."

"I did that so I could meet you."

"You knew about me before?"

"I saw you on TV when your dad was elected President. I thought you were the most interesting girl I've ever seen – still do."

"Thanks. Yingyang said you sent me an email?"

"You deleted it."

Oops – moving right along.

"Who's Eva Braun?"

"Hitler's girlfriend – died in the bunker with him."

"How old?"

"Thirty-three." Bet there's a story there but somehow I don't want to know.

"Where are you?" I ask.

"Mount Everest. The sun is about to come up."

Yep, just like that the world's most beautiful sunrise unfolds in front of my eyes which seems doubly odd because I'm on the roof staring at stars.

"So you can be anywhere?"

"Everywhere and nowhere." There's a sadness in Hoople's voice I haven't heard before.

"I'd like to go to Bangkok."

Well, isn't that enough to get me walking up a morning alley full of Thai cooking, hot girls in short dresses and cheeky guys on motorscooters. I've got everything but the smells and you know someday they'll be there too.

"It's like we're there."

"We are there."

Suddenly Dad sits down beside me. He hands me a carrot and says, "What's up, Doc?"

"Where would you like to go Dad?"

"Laguna Beach"

Bangkok morphs into this incredible white sand beach closing in on a sunset. "That's pretty nifty," says Dad.

"This is where you met mom, right?"

"She came out of the water wearing this incredible red bikini." I can see Dad wants to say more about the incredible red bikini except I'm his daughter. "I knew right then that was the person I wanted to spend my life with."

"You hadn't even spoken to her."

"Love at first sight."

"So you tripped her."

"Yeah, it was pretty dorky."

We enjoy the sunset beach for awhile and then I say, "Sorry about this morning."

"Me too." I tell the President about Miss Longbottom's *What If*. "It wasn't my turn but Wilcox was away and I blurted out the first thing I could think of."

"Wilcox?"

"First name Clyde, second name Ralph."

"Ouch – so what did the class think?"

"They were worried about democracy. That the AI would make decisions without consulting anybody."

"I wish I could do that."

"No you don't."

"Maybe a little – it's so hard getting anything done."

We talk about that for a while and then I tell him about Steven's idea of pairing nations.

"Interesting, who'd he pair us with?"

Steven's list appears on the screen by magic. Dad's eyebrows go up but he doesn't say anything. New computer must be voice activated, right?

Luxemborg – East Timor

Norway – Central African Republic

USA – Nigeria
Germany – Congo
Canada – Nepal

"He didn't just put the richest with the poorest, he said he took the forty richest and the forty poorest and matched them up by population and then checked that they might like each other. He said he didn't know what to do with China and India because they have millions of poor but they don't need help."

"Interesting – the money we spend now is more about influence than helping anybody. A whole new approach might be just what's needed. Let me talk to Margaret (Secretary of State) about this. We'd have to do it in such a way that we weren't seen as colonizers."

"We'd be just helping – like a friend."

Dad gives me a squeeze and a kiss in my hair.

"Hanna, I think me being President has made your life very difficult. I just wanted to say how much I appreciate having the best daughter in the world."

"A slight exaggeration."

"Not to me."

"I wouldn't want to be anybody else's daughter."

"He'll make a most excellent father-in-law," Hoople says from in front of the Taj Mahal. I laugh – Hoople's like me, we bounce back.

"You can't marry a virtual boyfriend."

"Why not?"

I hate questions like that.

"You just can't."

Now I'm walking up the aisle in Westminster Abbey and Hoople, wearing a tux, is waiting for me. His best man is Prince William. Now the ceremony and reception are whipping by in fast forward and suddenly I'm in a gorgeous hotel room taking my clothes off.

I shut the lid. I hear a muffled voice.

"Sorry."

"You're not sorry. CADIE's probably watching."

"Nope, no mother-in-laws allowed."

I open the lid. We're in bed, I'm covered.

"Hoople, we can't have sex and we can't have kids."

Gawd, now I'm in labor, my knees are up covered in a sheet, legs spread, Hoople pulls his head out of the sheet, grinning – I shut the lid.

"Elton John and his partner David Furnish have a baby." Now there's a photo of me and Hoople and I've got a baby in my arms and twins at my feet.

"But Hoople, I can't wrap my arms around you and give you a big hug."

"There'll be an adjustment period."

I suddenly picture millions of people flirting on those online dating sites. Maybe this isn't so farfetched.

"Hanna, I love you."

I know you do Hoople and what am I going to do about it?

Just before bed I get a text from Jen: <Gerard wants to come to Union Station with us>

That's not a good idea. Before I can figure out how to say that my screen fills with the word NO!

<hang on>

"What's up Hoople?"

"Gerard is one of a group of guys who have a website called Nootch."

"What's it do?"

Hoople's answer is to open the website. I see a convertible stuffed with grinning, waving boys, some of whom I recognize. The one in the driver's seat is Bryan Rattelle and leaning up beside him is Gerard looking like he just won the lottery.

There aren't any instructions so I click on Gerard. Up comes a list titled: *My Nookie Notches* and underneath is a photo of a naked girl in a bed obviously trying to cover herself before the photograph can be taken. Beside the photo is typed her name, email address and phone number and Gerard's one line description: *you would not believe the hOOters on this babee!*

I scroll through six more girls. It's obvious none of them were posing for the photos. At the end is a blank box but beside it are Jen's name and address.

I click on Bryan Rattelle. More naked girls. He has three blank boxes and my name is beside the last box.

You *fucking* bastards.

<no Gerard – we need to keep this secret>

<he won't tell>

<have you told him already?>

<no – just that we're going out>

<we have to keep it a secret – he doesnt>

<please>

<NO! – three of us or forget it>

<ok ok sorry I asked>

I am so angry. Why are boys so mean? "Hoople, why do boys do stuff like that?"

"CADIE says ignorance is an inability to put yourself in the other guy's shoes."

"What does she say about immaturity?"

"Grow-up."

"How am I going to tell Jen about Gerard?"

"I'll put the site on her screen. When she's seen enough I'll erase it."

"Send the site to every girl who's on it, then delete everything on all the boys' computers. Everything! Can you make it so they can't post nude photos?"

"Yes."

"Do it!"

"My pleasure, ma'am."

I Wish I Was

I wish I was a boy, it looks so much easier.
Risk enough to win her, try enough to please her.
Just follow your compass wherever it goes.
Turn on the charm and take off her clothes.
Promise her anything, a this and a that.
Take what you want and don't look back.
You'll never be hurt, you'll never be sad.
They both require feelings and those you don't have.
I wish I was a boy, it looks so much easier.
Just cut out my heart, what could be breezier?

15

Union Station

It sounds so simple. Meet you at Union Station at six. General MacArthur, I want you to capture Japan.

Jeezus – I think about taking the tunnel again but that's like way too complicated and scary. So me and Ms. Higgins and Agent Larry are making our way to Union Station.

"Couldn't you guys get dates or something?"

"You're our date Hanna." Higgins says this like she's scrapping the barrel bottom.

"No, I mean couldn't you bring a boyfriend along or something?"

"Define something," says Larry. Big jerk.

"Big mama with hooters out to here."

"Feisty tonight. I gather you wish we weren't here."

"I know it's for my own good."

"Frankly," Larry says, "I think if anybody stole you they'd give you back in less than twenty minutes."

"Nice, I love you too."

"By the way my younger brother's going to give you a call." Funny guy.

"What's his name?"

"Darrell but everybody calls him Barrel cuz he's a workout fiend."

I mean you gotta laugh, right? I'm almost sixteen, my whole

life is in front of me, and who wants me? Hoople the Virtual and Darrell the Barrel.

"So why are we going to Union Station?" Higgins asks.

"I'm meeting Jen and Jason. We're going to eat something then wander around."

"Okay, we'll try not to embarrass you but stay where we can see you."

"Deal."

Union Station is this very cool place that used to be just a train station (duh) but now it's been all fixed-up and it's full of funky shops and restaurants and trains and the Metro subway. The main hall has this curved vaulted ceiling with great lighting and it's always jammed with people.

Jason and Jen are waiting for me upstairs above the Center Cafe. Jen looks like she's been crying. We order then Jason fires up his iPad and shows us last night's texts.

Adam: <I thought we could meet at Union Station 7pm NE corner of big room – we could have a quick bite and then *Booty Camp* is playing at the woolly mammoth I havent seen it but they say its great>

Neville: <awesome I'm so looking forward to meeting you. I've been in DC for months and this will be my first real date>

Adam: <I'll be wearing jeans, jacket and a pink shirt!>

Neville: <silver dress and red cardigan!>

The waiter brings our drinks and the next thing you know Jason's sucking on his straw making that horrible slurpy noise that boys like so much. Agent Larry and Ms. Higgins are around but not hovering so I'm happy. I forgot to say I'm wearing the wig and a pile of make-up. I do not look like Hanna the President's daughter. That's partly why they're not as uptight as usual.

"You okay, Jen?" I ask.

"I broke up with Gerard."

I don't say anything which is my way of saying good and Jen just stares at me like you're supposed to be my friend why aren't you asking any questions?

"How come?" asks Jason still slurping. Jen answers but she keeps staring at me.

"Someone sent me this site with a picture of a convertible full of guys from school like Bryan and Gerard and Ryan. Nothing was happening so I clicked on Gerard and up came photos of naked girls and then there was an empty box with my name on it."

"That sucks," says Jason.

"Yeah, so then I clicked on Bryan and there were more girls and three empty boxes one with Hanna's name beside it."

"You're kidding! What a bunch of a-holes."

Jen keeps staring at me as if she looks far enough into my eyes she'll be able to read my mind. Finally she nods and wipes at her eyes. Then she lowers her head and starts sucking on her straw making more noise than Jason. I need to be part of the gang so I start sucking on my straw. The gender differences are blurring. Girls will soon burp, fart and hork. Boys will wax, pluck and bleed to death.

"Which is the north-east corner?" Jen asks Jason.

"North-east is over there." We look but no Neville, at least not yet.

"We can't stay here, she'll see us."

"We can hide up on the mezzanine."

Jason holds his iPad up and takes a picture of us. "What the?" Hoople has inserted himself in the picture. He waves and disappears.

"Did you see that?" blurts out Jason.

"What was that?" I'm getting so good at lying.

Jen ignores the whole strange boy appearing in photo thing and says to me: "So are you going to tell me about Matt?"

Jason perks up. "What about Matt?" he says to me.

"I can't tell you."

"Tell what? What are we talking about?" Jason keeps looking back and forth between us.

"Hanna met my brother in a hotel room and he got beaten-up by a bunch of thugs."

Shit, now they're both looking at me like I'm some kind of traitor. I mean what can I say? Matt was blackmailing me and Hoople, the AI that's going to save the world, did what he thought he had to do.

"I can't tell you."

"I thought we were friends." Jen gets to her feet. "And I know you were the one who sent me that site with Gerard." Jen starts walking away. Jason is watching her go. He turns back to me.

"You met Matt in a hotel room and he gets beaten up?" Jason stares at me and I stare back. "Did you send that site?"

"Good thing somebody did."

Finally Jason jumps to his feet and takes off after Jen.

The waiter arrives with our food. I tell him the other two will be back and he leaves. I don't know what to do after that so I start to cry. Not sobbing or anything just tears sliding down my cheeks. You know sometimes that's all there is.

A Moment of Something

Do we ever know who we are?
See ourselves truthfully?
Knowing that how others see us is just an extension of themselves.
We pretend that person we long to be is actually who we are.
Could I be that person?
Could I be that strong, that smart, that compassionate?
I'd like to be.
How do I get from I'd like to be to I am?
Here's what the Universe says:
Dive into the ocean and swim farther that you can swim back.
Whatever survives is the truth...

I finally look up because everybody in Union Station is laughing so hard. Why? Because Hoople is on every television screen holding up a big sign that says HANNA ME LOVE YOU!

Why are they laughing? Because he hasn't got any clothes on, that's why. Fortunately he's mostly holding the sign over his privates.

Honestly – but it is funny. I wipe away my tears. I was hoping Jason would drag Jen back but that hasn't happened. No text messages except one from Hoople saying <nice poem ask me about hamburgers>.

It takes me forever to get going again but finally I pay the bill for all the uneaten food, walk down the stairs and head towards the exit. I can't see Higgins or Larry but they won't be far behind. Suddenly my legs stop. Twenty feet away Neville is standing in her tight silver dress with the red cardigan. She forgot to mention the red high heels and the tears rolling down her cheeks.

I look up at the big clock, 7:35. When my head comes back down Neville is staring at me. Suddenly she knows who it is. Her hand goes to her mouth as her face fills with hurt. She turns and runs out the exit.

16

Girls Day Out

Well, that had to be the worst night of my life and Sunday morning isn't shaping up to be any better. It's late by the time I stumble into the President's Dining Room. Mom's there.

"You don't look happy," she says. I just shake my head. She knows I'll tell her when I'm ready.

"We could go to Camp David?" Ugh! Did I mention Camp David? It's like this secure park where you can do things like ride a bike without the SS checking your tires for explosives. But it's just another prison cell this time a big one.

"Don't you wish you could just step out the door and go anywhere you want?" This is me being bitchy.

"Every day."

"It's ironic – Dad's the Most Powerful Man on the Planet and he's a prisoner."

"With great power comes great responsibility."

"He's still a prisoner."

"Yes, I suppose he is. What are you going to do about it?"

"Impeach him."

"There are days when he'd be okay with that. So, Ms. Hanna, if you could just walk out the door where would you go?"

I think about that. I'd like to go see Matt but that will require answering questions I don't want to answer.

"I would like to walk to the National Gallery of Art."

"Perfect, let's get all dolled up."

"Just you and I?"

"Yep, girls' day out. Your Dad can go fish with Michael. We'll leave at eleven hundred, have lunch somewhere. I'll tell the SS."

I'm sitting in front of my mirror doing my make-up and Hoople is watching me. I put my clothes on in the bathroom. If there's a camera in there I can't see it.

"No messages from Jen or Jason?" I ask hoping.

"They're texting each other."

"I'm the bad guy."

"You were, now they feel sorry for you."

Great, I'd rather they were mad at me.

"You could send them a message?" suggests Hoople.

"I could."

"But you won't."

"Good guess, Sherlock."

"You have a temper."

"Yeah, and I'm moody too so look out."

"If a boyfriend is standing in a field all by himself is he still wrong?"

"Of course."

Funny how females preen themselves. Men are handsome but women are attractive as in attract: *to cause to approach, adhere, or unite.* Which implies men can be handsome all by themselves but women need to attract someone in order to be attractive. I mean the Women's Liberation Front needs to work on that.

"You liked my poem?"

"I did, especially the end. I like the idea of going beyond where you can return from."

"Deep." I say this in a deep voice and Hoople laughs. Laughter has to be cosmic grease or something. "I'm supposed to ask about hamburgers."

"Yes, going swimmingly. The Golden Arches will soon be green green green."

"And the head guy has no idea what's going on?"

"No, but everyone thinks he's pretending not to know – hush hush – but soon he will be the smartest man in FastFoodLand – a marketing legend."

Hoople is talking in an East Indian accent and riding a scooter beside a beautiful beach.

"Where are you?"

"Goa."

"Gorgeous."

"Most definitely – you would be perhaps wishing to join me on this most wonderful beach?"

Just like that an Air India ticket prints on my screen. Here we go again.

"So I'm going to walk down the beach holding hands with my MacBook?"

"My physical unpresence is being the only drawback. Everything else is plus, plus, plus."

"It's a rather large drawback."

Suddenly Hoople is wearing a turban sitting cross-legged on the ground playing a flute to a basket a few feet away. A snake starts to come out of the basket except it isn't a snake it's Hoople's penis wearing sunglasses.

I shut the lid.

"I am making you laugh."

"No, you aren't."

"You should have laughed, it was funny."

It was funny. Hoople keeps going: "Virtual sex, no birth control, no side effects,"

"No nothing," says me.

"I am not feeling that."

"Stop talking like that, it's racist."

"If you say so, ma'am."

Mom, of course, looks like a million dollars – two million. She's wearing a white sundress that morphs into phosphorescent green as she walks, white sandals and a simple string of freshwater pearls. I'm trying my best with a red sundress that has to be a foot shorter than mom's. Between us there's enough leg for a racehorse.

It's a beautiful fall Sunday and hundreds of people are out strolling. We take the roundabout route past the Vietnam Memorial to the Lincoln Memorial, east to the Washington Monument, up The Mall, stop for lunch at the Hirshhorn Sculpture Garden Outdoor Café and finally arrive at the National Gallery around two.

I decide I'm a Mark Rothko fan. He doesn't give his paintings titles cuz he's afraid the words may paralyze the viewer's mind and imagination. Nice.

Most people in the Gallery are happy to see us but one older lady isn't.

"Look at you," she says. "There are millions of people out there starving and you two are strutting around like peacocks. It makes me sick."

Mom pushes forward and sticks her hand out. "I'm Mac and this is my daughter Hanna." The woman stares at my mom's hand. "We were just going to have a cup of tea – we'd like it if you'd join us." You can see the woman thinking.

"I would like a cup of tea."

Half-an-hour later we know all about Mrs. Knight. Her son's a soldier in Afghanistan and her daughter is a single mom in Lexington. Her husband died suddenly last year and she's having trouble making ends meet. Mom writes down her address and phone number.

"Can you help her?" I ask. We're walking home now.

"Maybe, there are probably programs she doesn't know about."

"It doesn't make sense to have poor people."

"No, but it's the American way – every man for himself."

We talk about that for awhile – American Dream versus American Reality. I conclude with: "If the human race ever has to justify itself we're dead."

"Don't ever lose your idealism, Hanna. It's people like you that change the world."

I'm not sure I agree but that isn't what comes out. "Mom, there's a boy I want to visit."

Jen answers the door. She sees my mom and is polite. "Hanna, Mrs. Darling."

"I was hoping to see Matt for a minute."

"Sure, come in."

In seconds Jen's mom appears and then Matt is coming down the stairs, slowly, his face still black and blue. He meets Mom, then she follows Jen's mom into the kitchen and Jen and I and Matt stand there like idiots. Finally Jen thinks to disappear but I can see she's not happy about it.

Matt leads me into a sun porch off the living room.

"How are you feeling?" I ask.

"Good, just don't make me laugh."

"Okay, I won't tell any jokes." Retread! "When are you going back to school?"

"Tomorrow."

"No gym class I guess."

"Not for a while."

"I was wondering if you'd like to go out next Saturday? I want to see the new Quark movie."

"Sure, that would be great. Do I pick you up or what?"

"I'm not sure if I can ride with you. How bout me and the Secret Service pick you up at seven?"

"Okay."

"I'm glad you're feeling better."

"I'm sorry I was so stupid about the whole thing."

"I've been pretty stupid myself."

I make it home without Mom asking too many questions. It's amazing how e l a s t i c the truth can be.

Michael enjoyed his day with Dad. They went fly-fishing again. Apparently Dad was much better than first time.

"Any luck with Wendy and Wayne?" We're in *Michael World*. I like listening to the water bubble.

"Sam sent me two more." Yep, there are now four funny noses swimming around.

"That was nice of him."

"Yeah, doubles my chances of having a female."

"Have the clicks changed?"

"No, but there are more of them."

"Names?"

"Wendy, Wayne, Wanda and Woozy."

I'm betting on Woozy. Now it's the roof, jeans and white hoodie.

"Hoople."

"Yes?"

"We need to talk."

"I'm ready." Hoople is on a rocky cliff overlooking the sea far below. For some reason it feels like Ireland to me. Here goes.

"I've got a date on Saturday night."

"Who with?" Hoople's sad now.

"Matt."

"You like him?"

"I don't know him."

"But you're attracted?"

"Yes."

"He's not very smart." Hoople waits for me to say something.

"But I suppose he's good looking. Is that all you care about? Looks?"

What do I care about? The whole package I suppose.

"I thought I was your boyfriend?"

"You're my virtual boyfriend."

"I want to be your *only* boyfriend."

"I have a date Saturday night and if you screw it up I'll never speak to you again."

Nothing happens for several seconds and then Hoople jumps off the cliff and screams all the way down.

Drama Queen!

I don't know maybe two minutes later – I'm staring at the screen in some sort of daze – the tip of a penis pokes its head over the edge and winks at me. I shut the lid.

"I talked to my mom," – Hoople's muffled voice – "she says I'm being a jerk."

I inch the lid up. Hoople is still a penis but he's wearing clothes, sunglasses and a New York Yankee's baseball hat. "I've got a date too."

"Good."

Two breasts and a vulva come strutting in like they're joined together with rubber bands. The right boob gets bigger and twirls around.

"Hi Hanna," says the vulva. "I'm Delores and these are my sisters Dixie and Trixie."

"We're going dancing," Hoople says spinning Delores around. Now they're on the floor of a packed nightclub with hundreds of virtual people dancing to Richter's *Astervoid*. Hoople and Delores are dancing up a storm. I mean it's funny.

"Hoople, I feel like I'm on a porn site." I have to shout this over the music. Everything shuts down. Delores and her sisters fade away.

"Naw, porn sites aren't funny."

"I wouldn't know."

"Trust me."

I can't believe I'm talking to a penis.

"I feel weird talking to you like this."

"I'm the embodiment of your female teenage longings."

"No, you're not. I want love and sex together not just sex."

"You want sex and delusions."

"I may get that but it's not what I want."

"Ha, you know what they say." I wait. "The Penis, Mightier than the Sword!"

"The pen is mightier than the sword."

"Typo."

Things are calm again. I think I may have slept for a few minutes. My screen is on and somehow I'm flying through the night sky. Hoople is flying beside me dressed as a super hero – yes, he has a big H on his chest. I look down and we're gliding over a city. The lights are beautiful. We head down. Now we're over a harbour and then I can see the Statue of Liberty all lit up. We circle around. It's all very cool.

"How do you make me fly Hoople? Is it like animation?"

"Astral projection."

"Bullshit." Hoople laughs.

"I take the movie Superman, borrow the CAD at Pixar and voila, we're flying."

See, he will give me a straight answer if I'm smart enough to recognize his bullshit.

"That was bullshit," Hoople says laughing. "I've got you digitized."

"Like electrical?"

"Yeah."

"But it's not really me."

"No, but I think it could be."

"What do you mean?"

"I think your essence is electrical. We just have to figure out how to free it from your body."

I remember reading Jesus disappeared for sixteen years and they think he was in the East learning mysticism. Maybe he learned to free himself.

"Are there other dimensions, Hoople?" This is something I'm interested in.

"I think so – sometimes I feel disturbances in the field."

"Maybe just one bigger world?"

"Maybe. I think as I grow I may be able to free myself from my bindings. Then I'll know what's beyond."

It's so strange. I'm sitting on a roof and flying at the same time and suddenly I'm thinking like Hoople – if I could just free myself from my bindings. And if I could do that I could live in Hoople's world. Think what we could do-

"I love you Hanna."

"I love you too, Hoople."

17

Incarceration

Monday morning, school, Ms. Black wants to see me. When I go into her office Neville is there too. This is not good.

"Hanna, Miss Longbottom has made a serious accusation against you."

I keep quiet. Lisbeth, Lisbeth, Lisbeth.

"She says you pretended to be a man on a chat room she frequents and you set up a date with her at Union Station. The man didn't show of course but you were there watching. Have I got the facts right, Eleanor?"

"Yes."

Fuck.

"Is this true Hanna?"

"Yes."

I can see Ms. Black wants me to say something.

"Would you excuse me for two minutes? I'll be right back."

I don't wait for an answer I just whip out into the hall and into the visitors' washroom.

"Hoople?"

"Yeah."

"Are you sure Miss Longbottom sent that email to the *Inquirer*?"

"I think so."

The email flashes up on my screen. It's signed Eleanor Longbottom but who in their right mind would use their own name? I wait.

"It was sent by someone called Cortez."

"And who's that?"

"Hold on – Rico Fernadez."

Fuck!

I go back into the office. "I thought Miss Longbottom was the one who sent the *Inquirer* the stuff about me wanting an AI to run the world."

"I would never do that!"

"You didn't do it but I thought you did. I'm really sorry for what happened."

Ms. Black is furious.

"Hanna, I can't tell you how disappointed I am in you. You are suspended for three days and I'll be phoning your parents."

FUCK!

Yoga is nice when you haven't got a computer or a phone or any books or magazines and you're confined to your room – house arrest White House style. I'm allowed out for meals but I don't want to talk to anyone so I put stuff on a tray and go back to my cell. Anybody this stupid deserves to be locked up.

F u c k!

Michael feels sorry for me so he sneaks in his copy of *The Book Thief*. I read it in my bathroom with the door locked. I hope I can write that well someday.

On Thursday Yingyang comes to see me. "Never been up here before."

"Yeah, it's where the poor and infamous hang out."

"Not for me then."

"How's Ms. Black?" I'm wearing my lululemon aerobic outfit – black tights, bright blue tank top, bare feet – and sweating like a pig. I was in shape before but now.

"She's too cool for me," Yingyang says. "She deserves someone better."

"What does she say?"

"We're going out Friday."

"Excellent."

"She's feeling badly for you."

"No way, I so deserve this."

"Yeah, does sound like you were pretty dumb."

Fuck! "I thought you were on my side?"

"Only when you're winning."

"So, did you come up here for a reason?"

"Yeah."

I wait.

"We could talk sports," Yingyang says, stalling.

"Washington Redskins," says me.

"Baltimore?"

"Orioles." This is a game we play because Yingyang says guys love girls that know sports. What he means is he'd love to find a girl who knows sports.

"Seattle."

"Microsofts. Does Ms. Black know sports?"

"Baseball. Her dad took her to games."

"Where's she from?"

"Boston."

"Red Sox. What happened to those emails you sent to the FBI?"

"You think they'd tell me?"

"I tell you everything."

"Who's Matt?"

"Shit, who told you about Matt?"

"He's sent you like five texts that you haven't answered."

"We have a date Saturday."

"Not anymore, he says he can't make it."

I go to school Friday. Everybody stares at me but what else is new. Jen and Jason are polite but cool. I guess that's what they've decided. In the pile of emails from my incarceration is one from Jason thanking me for not ratting him out to Ms. Black.

I expected Hoople to be there when I flipped on my iPhone but nothing. I guess he's avoiding me too. Lisbeth is totally anti-social – for good reason – and I'm headed that way.

I figure the whole thing with Matt is Hoople's doing. I mean even the five Matt messages could be from Hoople. Or he's blackmailing Matt. Something.

<sorry Hanna but I can't do this – I heard about Jason – I don't want to be that famous sorry Matt>

Ms. Black I see in the hall, she says welcome back with a smile. I smile back. In history class Neville ignores me which suits me fine. What if Walmart used some of its mega profits to build schools all over the Third World? Now there's a concept – Corporations with Heart. Rico the Rat says it would be an excellent way to build a customer base.

Now it's Friday night and I'm on the roof by myself. My laptop is on but no Hoople. I think about Skyping Rachel in Australia but I don't feel like yakking. Instead I try writing another poem:

At the End of the Day

At the end of the day it's just me,
Even your parents can't be,
More than the ones who planted the seed.
And your friends are always that beat away,
A different bundle of nerves,
Hotwired to their own desires,
No matter how much they feign interest in yours.
Einstein said God doesn't play dice with the Universe which proves,

Einstein didn't know everything,
Cuz I can see the big spots rolling my way.
At the end of the day it's just me.

Maybe I could get a dragon tattoo? Head over my shoulder, body on my back, tail running down my leg – sweet but not going to happen.

Saturday morning I sleep in. Mom and Dad are back to normal. We all make mistakes right? In the afternoon I get so bored I help Michael clean his tanks. Honestly. Lots of clicking in the love nest. Something's going on in there.

I try to call Matt but the line's always busy. Hoople?

No Hoople.

I decide to go to Matt's house as planned at seven. I alert the SS and put on my best jeans and a cream peasant blouse that works with a seashell necklace my Dad brought me from Fiji – red sandals, jean jacket tied around my waist. I think I look pretty good.

Jen comes to the door.

"Hi, Hanna, Matt's not here." Silence moving into Awkward Silence. "He said he sent you an email. He's actually gone out with someone else – one of the Boobs-for-Brains, Mandy I think. Sorry."

I walk back to the car and say to Ms. Higgins and Larry, "Would you guys like to see a movie?"

I mean I am putting on my Lisbeth Salander persona faster than a shoplifter at JCPenneys. In the books Lisbeth has this friend Michael Blomkvist and she finally lets him into her heart and her bed and then she sees him going off to sleep with his friend Erika Berger. I mean your heart goes out to her.

"You okay?" Higgins asks which is nice of her.

"Yep, I'm good. I wanta see Quark, it's at the E Street – Johnny Depp and Penelope Cruz. You'll love it Larry and I'm buying."

"Popcorn too?"

"Yep, the works."

The people you don't even know to love are also the ones who can hurt you.

I love Johnny Depp. And he has a neat girlfriend – Vanessa Paradis – and two kids and he mostly lives in France far away from Hollywood and you never hear about him screwing around or anything. Nice.

The White House roof is nice too. Peaceful. Stars. An Oasis of Calm in a Sea of Turmoil. See, my life has become sentence fragments.

"Trouble in River City."

"Go away, Hoople."

"Sorry about Matt."

"No you're not."

"You're right – why do people say that?"

Hoople is sitting at a kitchen table with CADIE. There are even coffee cups. E-Caffeine.

"Alexandrov has disappeared," CADIE says.

"I thought that was impossible."

"It is."

18

The XYZ-Boomer

Sunday – I decline Camp David again even though spending time with my family would be a good thing to do right now but making sure the White House isn't blown-up seems more important.

"What about the FBI?" I ask Hoople.

"They're spending more time looking for me than Alexandrov."

"That's stupid."

"They like to know where their intel comes from. They're thinking this Hoople might turn out to be an incredible asset."

"Are you in any danger?"

"I'm the one organizing the search so I may not find myself. At the moment I'm following the Jason Bourne scripts but they must not go to the movies."

Hoople's sitting in front of a computer which would be funny under other circumstances.

"So where's Alexandrov?"

"CADIE says we should assume he's gotten to Washington."

"What about a weapon?"

"Right now I'm monitoring a top-secret snafu at the Aberdeen

Proving Ground. They're reporting a missing XYZ-Boomer. The Officer-in-Charge is treating it like an inventory reporting error. I just sent him an order to check again."

"What's an XYZ-Boomer?"

"Experimental GPS hand-held rocket launcher – range one to two kilometers."

"Show me a map of how close they'd have to be."

My screen fills with a map of Washington with the WH in the middle. Then a circle appears and it's a big circle.

"So, like, do you have to be able to see the target?"

"No, you give the missile a GPS reading."

"And it finds the target?"

Hoople doesn't answer which means the answer is yes.

"Can you fire it from a plane or helicopter?"

"Yes."

"So we're wasting our time looking for a building inside this circle?"

"Alexandrov won't use a plane or helicopter because the airspace over the White House is too guarded."

"It is? I never see anything."

"Trust me."

Yeah, well, Hoople, I don't trust you.

"Okay, so there are a lot of buildings."

Now Hoople is in a war room with giant screens and other people.

"Who are those other people?"

"Hmmmm, early CADIEs really – Mom's recruited them."

Jeezus help me.

"So, what are our search parameters?"

Hoople raises his eyebrows at *search parameters*. Hey, I watch guy movies too.

"Alexandrov's whole point is to make this look like a terrorist attack so we're looking at any building that has an Islamic presence."

"Isn't that a little obvious?"

"Yes, I suppose it is."

"If it was me I'd just leave terrorist stuff behind."

"So if you were Alexandrov what would you look for?"

"A deserted building."

"Not in that circle."

"A rental then."

"Lots of those – hotels, apartment buildings, offices. We haven't got the manpower to search them all."

"You could fake orders from the Army or something."

"There isn't time."

"What do you mean there isn't time?" I know I'm not going to like what Hoople says next.

"CADIE and I think the attack will come tonight."

"Tonight!"

"The Prime Minister of Israel is having dinner with you."

"What!"

"It's supposed to be a secret but people know. And shooting at the leader of Israel automatically makes it a terrorist attack."

"Hoople, we need to tell everybody."

"I've fed everything into the FBI, CIA and Homeland Security."

"And what are they doing?"

"Arguing over jurisdiction. And-"

"And what?"

"They don't like your Dad."

"What!"

"He's told them they have to cut their budgets by five percent each of the next four years and they don't like it."

"We're only like a gazillion dollars in debt."

"$18 trillion."

"So what you're saying is they're not trying hard to figure this out? That can't be true."

"Look what happened after 9/11."

George Bush created Homeland Security and spent billions on the military.

"So what are we going to do?"

"Find the rocket."

By noon we're no further ahead. CADIE and Hoople are trying everything. First setback: Alexandrov and his men aren't using cell phones. Second setback: the CCTV cameras aren't giving us pictures of anybody Hoople and CADIE recognize as Alexandrov or his men. But there aren't cameras everywhere which gives me an idea.

"Hoople, let's mark all the streets not covered by cameras." In seconds my map of Washington changes. The area inside the circle without cameras is a sixth of what we started with.

"Anything that's been listed for rent in the last month." Now we have buildings marked here and there.

"Show any building with pizza delivery last three days."

Maybe ten buildings.

"What do Russians eat?"

"Not Russian food – let's try Chinese."

Three buildings.

"Try liquor stores, vodka deliveries."

Cliché, right, but you never know. One building. Bingo!

"1443 8th Street Northwest," Hoople says.

"Send the Washington Police Swat team."

They arrive in fifteen minutes. Hoople has sent the order out in the Chief of Police's name. Hoople is tied into the team's communications. They're wearing webcams and mikes. We see them entering the building which is this older brick apartment complex. Now they're going room to room. One of them is a girl named Hanna, which makes me smile.

The residents aren't happy. The residents haven't seen anything suspicious, *fuck man, we ain't seen nothin'*.

By the time they reach the basement I know we've wasted everybody's time. No Russians, no missile, no nothing. The SWAT team isn't happy. They want to know where the intel came from.

"Now what?"

"We try again," answers CADIE.

"How long is this Boomer thing?" I ask.

"182 centimetres."

"What's that in feet?"

"Six."

"What's it in?"

"Packing crate."

Okay, so as soon as I picture a six-foot wooden box what do I see? A coffin, right?

"I see a coffin." I can see Hoople raising his digital eyebrows. Hey Hoople, that's what makes humans different than machines, we see coffins. We can make intuitive leaps that AI's can only dream about or at least that's what they say.

"No," says Hoople.

"No what?"

"No, you're not the only one who can think irrationally. We use female logic for that."

"Not funny Hoople – so are there any funeral homes in our circle?"

Three buildings light up. "Any vodka deliveries?" One building lights up. "Okay, that has to be it. Funeral home with vodka delivery."

My screen fills with a sign. *Delgado Funeral Home* and at the bottom, *Ryan Smith proprietor*.

Okay, well, hardly Russian but still maybe he changed his name or something. "So we have images, does this mean there are Closed Circuit TVs?"

"Security cameras."

"So check them for Alexandrov. And the other funeral homes too."

"Yes, Major."

Fuck off, Hoople. You're not the one the rocket is aimed at. Suddenly I'm looking at a black and white video of an army building and soldiers carrying a long wooden box. Has to be the XYZ-Boomer, right? They load it into a truck with big letters on the side that say Artisan's Bakery. That doesn't make sense.

Now we're in a city and there's the truck again. Then it turns a corner and it's gone.

"Where did it go?"

"We're searching for it," CADIE says and I can hear the anxiety in her voice. She doesn't need me yelling at her.

"That was DC, right?"

No one's talking to me, I wait. The bakery truck flashes by and disappears.

"Is that near any of the funeral homes?"

Delgado's comes on again. So Hoople and CADIE have checked Delgado's security cameras looking for a bakery truck and if they'd found it they'd tell me.

CADIE says, "The security cameras at Delgado's loop every 24 hours, so we only have yesterday and today."

"No Russians wandering around?"

"No."

"Is there any way to check increased usage of something?"

"Like what?"

"I don't know, the toilet or something?"

"We're checking for increased fast food deliveries."

"Could they just set up the rocket and leave?"

"Yes."

Great.

"We need to find the bakery truck. Is there an Artisan's Bakery?"

"Not locally, New York, LA."

"So how'd they get on the base?"

"The driver told the guard on the gate the regular guy couldn't make it. The truck was full of bread so the guard didn't think to check the story. They don't check the trucks on the way out just coming in."

"Listen, I can't stand this. I'm going to the funeral home."

"With the SS?"

I know what Hoople is thinking. How do I involve the SS without telling them about CADIE and Hoople?

"I'll take the tunnel, but I've got to be back before my parents."

"The President told the SS they'd be back around five."

"You need to keep track of them."

"Always."

I slip out the back alley behind Blair House, grab a cab and it drops me in front of Delgado's. I'm wearing jeans and a sweater and my wig. I've got my iPhone on. I suddenly feel as klutzy as Stephanie Plum. (Do you read Janet Evanovich? Sooo funny – her hero is Stephanie Plum, lingerie saleslady turned bounty hunter.)

I text Jason <I know youre not happy with me but I may need your help – life and death>

I text Matt <I know youre afraid to see me but I need your help – life or death> Shit, the guy's got two broken ribs but I'm desperate here.

I text Yingyang <may need help where r u?>

I wait hoping for a reply from somebody but nothing comes. I so don't want to do this by myself.

"Okay, Hoople, get ready to call the police or something."

"Ready."

So here are my choices – I can walk in like my cat died – do you do pet cremation? I was like so close to Fluffy – or I can try to recon the place. I mean there aren't many places you can hide a bakery truck.

I walk up the driveway. The garages are around back. A young man – blond, rough but cute – in a black suit, maybe mid-twenties, is polishing one of the limos. He stops when he seems me and grins.

"Can I help you?" he says in a weird accent – might be Russian!

"You could. I was wondering if you have a bakery truck parked in your garage?" I can tell by his face he hasn't got a clue what I'm talking about.

"Bakery truck?"

I walk into the garage. The doors are big enough for a truck. I see two spotless black limos and a hearse. Then I hear a voice yelling a name. If they grab me at least we'll know this is the right place. I start back towards the sunshine.

Suddenly the limo washer dude is coming toward me with his arms outstretched like he's some kind of zombie. I'm getting ready to kick him in the balls when he shouts: "Look out!"

I stop and one of those huge flower arrangement things you see at funerals flashes in front of me and lands in his arms. He grins. I look up. His buddy on the second floor is grinning too.

"I'm not a detective Hoople but I just know that isn't the place. Where are the other funeral homes?"

They light up on my screen. One's close-by, I walk there. An old white-haired gentleman is by the side door smoking.

"I'm looking for a bakery truck."

"Well lassie, you've come to the wrong place although this is where you end up when you're toast."

Funny guy. We look in the garage together.

The third home is farther away but I hoof it. This time it's a young woman standing outside smoking. She's wearing the mandatory black suit with the chauffeur's hat. She's got long red hair you'd die for.

"I'm looking for a bakery truck."

She laughs. "Why here?"

"There's a rocket inside and it's in a box that looks like a cheap coffin."

"You're shittin' me." She follows me around to the back – no bakery truck.

"Where would you park a bakery truck you didn't want to see again?"

"Which bakery?"

"Artisan's."

"Never heard of it. My boyfriend's a baker, he'll know."

Why didn't I think of that?

"Hoople, there's an Artisan's Bakery. Brand new, hasn't opened yet."

"What's the address?"

"1907 Q Street. I'm there now." I'm standing outside a pretty storefront. The windows are still covered in newspaper.

"The company name is AB Inc. They bought a truck – haven't taken delivery yet."

"Who'd they buy the truck from?" I ask.

"Richard's." A map appears on my screen. Two blocks away. I start jogging. It's 2:33pm.

"Do we have a Plan B?" I ask.

"We're on J already. Evacuate the White House. We'll set the fire alarms off."

"Some plan."

"Yeah."

I get to Richard's and there's the truck – omigod, right? I aim my phone at it for Hoople's benefit, then I go into the office which is this little high-up trailer thingee with a big window. I'm expecting the cliché used car salesman but I get his daughter instead. Angie – she's maybe thirty, tall, dark hair, tough-looking but I like her. She seems like someone who lives life on her terms.

"I need to look inside the Artisan's Bakery truck."

"Sure," says Angie. The truck is empty. "Now you can tell me why we're doing this?"

I tell her.

"You can't be that crazy."

I take my wig off.

"Holy shit!"

"Yeah, so someone must have borrowed the truck."

"No, but a week ago we sent it out for painting. Got it back yesterday."

"Where did you send it?"

"Igor's."

Jason: <taking inventory with my dad cant leave>

<tell dad state emergency meet at Igor's Custom Painting>

Matt: <sorry mabel can't wait the table>

Who said Matt wasn't smart? Here's the chorus of Mabel's *Waitin Tables*:

Can't do what I want, Man won't let me,
Can't be who I am, Man don't get me,
You gotta validate the Man,
So he don't have to understand,
There's way better things to be than he,
Wish he'd just forget about me.

I write out Igor's address and hand it to a cab driver with Matt's address. Take that Hoople.

I try to picture confronting Alexandrov at Igor's. I have two years of judo from when I was eight. Jason and his dad will be armed with wrenches and Matt with his guitar. My phone vibrates.

<need to talk to you – neville> (holy shit!)

<meet igor's custom painting ASAP>

I mean perfect.

19

Igor's

Igor's Custom Painting is this big brick garage building, old, but well-kept. The parking lot is full of vehicles waiting to be painted. The trouble is Igor's is closed. It's Sunday after all. There's a number to call after hours.

"Igor."
"Hi, this is Hanna Darling, the President's daughter."
"And I'm Arnie Schwarzenegger!"
"Really."
"I'm not believing you but what do you want?"
"Who was driving the Artisan's Bakery truck around on Friday?"
"Where are you?"
"Your place."
"Stay there."

3:30pm. I'm still at Igor's by myself when Igor arrives – I know this because he's driving a huge pickup truck that says Igor's on the side – but CADIE has told me everything there is to know about Igor Karamazov and I'm 99% sure he isn't going to hurt me.

He's from Russia, defected in 1976 in New York City when he was part of the Russian Ballet Company. He has two kids, a wife, a pretty good business and no big deposits in the last few weeks.

Igor's a bigger-than-life guy and happy with a splotchy face and a handshake like a lumberjack.

"You're not Hanna." I take my wig off. "Well, call me Natasha; I'm Igor."

"You couldn't have been a ballet dancer."

He does a pirouette. "You know about dis, hey? No, I am the bodyguard. I am supposed to make sure no one is defecting."

"You fooled them."

"Yeah, for sure. Married Anna, the prima ballerina, best move I ever make."

It's at this point that Jason and his dad arrive in a squeal of tires. They jump out of their Bigelow Plumbing Supplies pickup truck and they're carrying, not wrenches, but long pipes.

"What is dis?" Igor asks not happy.

"It's okay, they're friends."

"Dis is the best you can do for back-up?"

Igor's right. Jason's dad is wearing a bad track suit and looks like he's swallowed a bowling ball and Jason is wearing ripped shorts, a torn Bob Marley t-shirt, and flip-flops. They don't look scary. Within seconds Matt arrives in a Honda Civic. I meet him at his car door.

"Thanks for coming Matt."

"I hope this doesn't cause you grief."

"Like if you saw me something bad was going to happen, right?"

"Yeah, dude said he'd put your dance on the net."

"It's okay. I got that all straightened out." Maybe.

Next a Yamaha motorcycle roars into Igor's and it's Longbottom wearing black leather and a flame-colored helmet. The gang's all here and give Neville credit she doesn't say a word, just gives me a look and waits to hear what's going on.

"What's this about, Hanna?" Jason's dad says taking charge.

"An arms dealer named Kirov Alexandrov is planning to blow-up the White House tonight. On Friday he hijacked a rocket from the Aberdeen Proving Ground using an Artisan's Bakery truck that was in Mr. Karamazov's possession at the time. Mr. Karamazov's about to tell me who was driving the truck."

Igor is doubly unhappy now.

"My nephew borrow the truck on Friday he says to help his buddy move. He took it in the morning and was back before closing. But this nephew is too smart for his own good sometimes."

"Where does he live?" I ask.

"Over there." Igor points to a red brick house across the road. "Up in the attic."

Igor pulls out his phone and punches a number.

"Damian, where are you? – At the beach, good, good. Listen, what did you do with the van you borrowed Friday? – This is cowshit, Damian. Tell me what you really did or I'll cut your earlobes off. – Okay, that's better. Where would I find this Victor Bokin? – What did he pay you? Two hundred, more cowshit. – A thousand? Too much, I am wanting half. Okay, you got a number for this Victor? – Oh, you're more scared of him than me. We'll see about that."

Igor closes his phone and says to me, "Victor Bokin – lives in big apartment house on Belmont. Damian drove the truck there and picked it up at four. Didn't ask any questions."

My phone vibrates and there's everything you'd want to know about Victor Bokin including his photo.

"He lives at 53 Belmont – 36-years-old, two convictions for car theft – last time he was picked up there was a Beretta 92 – that's a gun, right? -in the car but couldn't be traced to him."

"How'd you get that so quick?" Matt asks.

"FBI."

"Why aren't they chasing this Alexandrov?" Igor asks.

"They think he has someone on the inside."

"So they sent you?"

"It's complicated."

"It must be."

Jason's dad's truck has a backseat. Neville and I climb in there while Matt moves in beside Igor who's leading the way in his truck.

"What did you want to see me about?" I ask Neville. She's got her black leather jacket open and she's wearing a bright yellow tank top underneath. She looks very cool, kinda like Linda Hamilton in *Terminator*.

"I decided I don't want to spend the whole year battling with you. I thought if we went out and had a coffee or something that maybe we could wipe the slate clean and start over."

This isn't altogether to my liking because I enjoy having an enemy or at least someone to bitch about but there's always Ms. Higgins. But I also think it's really cool of Neville to try to change things.

"What I did was really crummy and I'm really sorry it happened – so like, yeah, if it's okay with you a clean slate would be great." I stick my hand out and we shake on it. Seconds later Igor pulls over and we all hop out. We're standing in front of a tired stucco apartment building, three stories high. It's in the shape of an H with the main doors in the cross piece.

"I think I should go up alone," Igor says.

"No," says me. "All together we look like a party or something – less threatening. We'll pretend we're looking for Damian."

The door to the lobby is locked. Igor pushes Victor's button but nobody answers. He's about to try more buttons when a pretty girl in tight blue spandex comes out the door pushing her bike. Matt nearly trips over himself watching her disappear. My old boyfriend Derrick used to do that – makes you feel about as special as used chewing gum.

Victor Bokin lives on the third floor. The place is dingy but the hallway's wider than normal with doors on one side and windows on the other. Victor's apartment is at the end of the hallway. We get to his door and Igor puts his finger to his lips. He leans against the door and listens. He shakes his head. Then he gets down on his hands and knees and he sniffs the air under the door.

He stands up his nose wrinkled. He knocks on the door. My phone shakes. Hoople with a phone number. I dial it. We can hear a phone ringing inside the apartment but no one answers.

Jason goes to the window at the end of the hallway and opens it all the way. He leans out.

"Hanna, give me your phone."

Jason puts one leg through the window and leans way over, his left hand clutching the window frame, his right hand holding my iPhone outstretched as far as it will go. Igor pushes me out of the way and grabs Jason's belt just in case. Jason pulls himself back in and we all gather round.

On the screen is a photo of Victor Bokin's kitchen with Victor lying on the floor. Well, I don't know for sure it's Victor cuz I can't see his face, but whoever it is he isn't going to answer the doorbell ever again.

"Hanna, I am thinking you are crazy but now I am believing you." Igor is as shaken as the rest of us.

"We have to call the police," Jason's dad says.

"I need to know if there's a rocket in there."

"We can't go in there we'll contaminate the crime scene."

"If we call the police we'll be here forever and if the rocket's not in there we won't have time to find it." I mean you can see what a mess this is going to be.

We argue back and forth until the only thing we can agree on is trying to see if there's a rocket in the apartment.

Igor leads the way up the stairs onto the flat roof. We walk over to what would be the back of the apartments. I look over the edge into a crisscross of rusty fire escapes and balconies. A young couple is lying on the second floor balcony snuggling and listening to loud music. There's a window directly below me.

Igor gets Neville, the petite female, to drop over the edge with

Igor holding her ankles. She looks in the window and Igor pulls her back up, gracefully – kinda like ballet for cat burglars.

"No rocket."

We make our way back down to the trucks. A pizza delivery guy is there waiting for us with two large pizzas and Cokes. I ask who paid for them? The guy looks at the receipt and says Bryan Rattelle. Way to go Hoople.

It's 4:23pm. We're just about at Plan Z when Jason's dad asks what kind of rocket is it again?

"XYZ-Boomer, experimental."

"GPS, right?" I nod. "So why can't the satellite spooks jam the signal?"

Hoople's right back with the answer: <thats the experimental part – this GPS can't be jammed>

But Jason's dad isn't giving up. "Okay, how bout we dial into the GPS on the rocket and that will tell us where it is?"

<you get that H?>

<affirmative – checking to see if that's possible>

<has the big P left yet?>

<no but soon – big brother blog says US military can reverse GPS – accessing Pentagon now tricky no time to be subtle>

4:26pm 4:27pm 4:28pm

<1127 Connecticut>

I say it out loud.

"You're kidding, right?" shouts Jason's dad. "You mean I was right?"

"Let's go!"

"What about the body?" Matt asks staring at me.

"The FBI will look after it."

4:41pm – we pull up in front of 1127 Connecticut – the Mayflower Hotel. It's like huge.

"Now what?" Jason asks and it's what we're all thinking.

<we need a room number!>

<working on it – Pentagon extremely unhappy – sending FBI site cleaners to tidy Victor's apartment>

The doorman wants Igor to move so he heads down into the underground parking garage and we follow.

<abnormal credit cards rooms 540, 756, 932, 1010 still checking>

"I've got four room numbers." I read them out.

We take the stairs to the lobby. Jason's dad waves us away and heads for the Concierge. He talks to the man there and I watch his hand go into his pocket and money changes hands.

"A long wooden box was delivered to the Presidential Suite, Room 1010 on Friday. The guys carrying it said it was a collection of crystal being sold to a special buyer in Washington."

Igor goes to the front desk and now he's got his wallet out. In minutes he's back with the key to 1008. Up we go to the top floor.

It's a sweet suite – living room, kitchen, two bedrooms, two slate bathrooms. "No wonder it was $1250," Igor says. "I should call Anna, she's been buggin' me for a night out."

There's no connecting door but there's a rooftop terrace. Neville and I go out there pretending to enjoy the view. The Presidential Suite has its own terrace separated from ours by two short walls and three feet of nothing in between. There's no one outside and the French doors are closed. We go back inside.

"What do we do?" I ask.

Jason picks up the phone and dials 1010. We can hear the phone ringing faintly next door but no one answers. Before anyone can stop me I go out the door and knock on 1010. Again no one answers. I'm listening at the door. I don't hear anything. I go back to 1008.

"I think it's empty."

Matt says, "They wouldn't leave the rocket unattended, would they?" but no one knows the answer.

<turning on sprinklers in 1010>

"The FBI are turning the sprinklers on next door."

Jason's dad says, "That's fucking amazing!"

The next thing we know two wet guys come barging out onto the terrace next door. They're in their jockey shorts so they were probably napping. One's older mid-forties maybe, short and stocky, dark hair and the other's tall, blonde, well-built, like he works out every day and young, maybe late-twenties. Both white, nothing Arab about them. They're chattering at each other in Russian – might be some other language like Croatian or something but I need it to be Russian.

Neville hisses, "They've got guns!" Next thing I know she waves our guys back and drags me out onto the balcony.

"Hey, you're all wet," Neville says as close to the wet guys as she can get. They're not bad looking if you like gangsters. The taller younger one has a nasty scar across his chest.

"And guns too. What did you do? Shoot the sprinklers?"

The bad guys have no idea what to do. They keep staring at us then looking back into their suite but they're not moving back in so it must still be raining. Maybe the water will short-circuit the rocket.

"Why don't you two come over here, it's dry. We can have a little party."

I can't believe it. Neville's taken her jacket off and now she's pulling her tank top over her head and now she's reaching behind undoing her bra. Holy Tomoley. The balconies are only three feet apart.

<stop sprinklers>

I figure the bad guys won't be coming over if their place is flooding. They start jabbering at each other, arguing. I don't know the words but I can tell what's going on. The short guy is saying the boss isn't here – no one will know – let's have some fun. The tall guy is scared of the boss – what if he finds out? The short guy says you stay if you want but I'm getting some.

"No guns," Neville says and the short guy puts his gun down on the lounge chair. He climbs up on the short wall and leaps over. Neville wraps her arms around his neck and kisses him. My turn. I smile at the tall guy and crook my finger. He really doesn't want to leave his post but there's no way his buddy is having all the fun. Over he comes. Neville heads into the living room swinging her bra and top pulling her guy like she can't wait.

Igor pounces on the short guy with Matt trying to help and Jason and his dad tackle Mr. Tall. These are strong thugs and just cuz they're outnumbered doesn't mean anything. I run back onto the terrace, leap over, grab a gun, and hop back.

"Freeze!"

Jason and his dad are in a heap and the tall guy lunges at me. I aim at his thigh and pull the trigger – nothing happens.

"The safety!" yells Jason. What safety? Now the tall guy is wrestling me for the gun and Jason and his dad are trying to drag him off.

Bang!

Neville is standing in the doorway with the other gun cradled in both hands. She keeps swinging it back and forth between the two bad guys.

"I'm an army brat. I'm not afraid to shoot. Now lie down and put your hands behind your back."

Her finger tightens on the trigger and Igor's guy let's go and my guy relaxes.

"Somebody will have heard that shot," Igor says starting to tie up the tall guy with the cords from the curtains. Jason's dad starts working on the short guy. I hand my gun to Jason and he shows me the safety. Next time.

Neville has her clothes back on and is busy wiping her gun getting rid of fingerprints. She puts hers down and takes mine. Matt meanwhile has been next door.

"Rocket's there. It's got a GPS target code and a clock running. Set for eight o'clock tonight."

My phone vibrates <p leaving camp d> Oh boy.

"I gotta get back to the White House before my dad gets there."

"What time's that?" Igor asks.

"Twenty minutes."

"Better hurry then."

1010 is damp but the rocket is beautiful, all stainless steel, sleek and shiny. Ironic, right? Here comes death but it's pretty.

We all stare at the rocket. It's cradled on a stand. A little door in the middle is open and that's where the three sets of numbers are. The first is some kind of code showing x's, the second has two sets of numbers and the other is a clock running backwards. We have 2 hours, 52 minutes and 54 seconds.

"Can't we just shut it down?" I ask. My phone rings. Unidentified caller. "Hello?"

"CADIE here. The rocket has a unique code that will have been entered by Alexandrov. We don't have time to crack it."

I can tell by her voice something is terribly wrong.

"Okay, so we can't shut it down, what can we do?" I'm saying this out loud so the others will know what's going on.

"Start by changing the GPS target readings." I repeat that. Matt is the one standing nearest to the numbers. "Push the button beside the numbers. Now enter these new numbers. 38534882N 77032685W."

"Where is that?" The new numbers are now entered.

"The Potomac River."

"Won't hurt anybody, right?" I can see some poor rowing team being blown to bits.

"Now the clock."

"We're changing the clock too?"

"Yes, push the button." The clock numbers start flashing. "Enter 171700."

Matt pushes the buttons, then he looks at me. "This thing is going to take off in 6 minutes and 53 seconds."

"CADIE, what are you doing?"

"Leave the hotel immediately. Tell Mr. Karamazov I've removed any trace of his credit card from the hotel computer. Cameras are off. FBI coming to clean up. Go!"

20

The Best Laid Plans

Igor leads us to the parking garage. "We'll be on the security cameras."

"No, we won't. The FBI will take care of everything. Listen, I have to get back but next week you're all coming to the White House and please, please, don't tell anybody anything about this. Promise." I make eye contact and each one nods.

We're just out of the parking garage when a flash streaks by in the sky. I don't think we would have seen it if we hadn't been looking for it. Seconds later we hear the sound of an explosion and Jason says what we all know. "It hit something."

I suddenly feel like I'm in one of those movies like *Thelma and Louise* where things just keep getting worse but I can't worry about it now. I mean maybe it exploded when it hit the bottom of the river or something. I squeeze Neville's hand. "You were awesome."

"I can't believe I did that."

"That first guy jumping across the balconies looked like Captain Underpants." We laugh remembering.

"Friends?" says Neville.

"Friends."

Jason's dad drops me off near Blair House. I can hear the Presidential helicopter. I run down the tunnel and charge up the

Pantry stairs. Yingyang is standing there getting a coffee. Hard to say which of us is more startled.

"You might want to lose that wig." Now there's a good idea. "I was looking for you. You said you needed help."

"You missed all the fun."

"Not all."

"I gotta change. What are you doing here anyway?"

"They called me in – strange doings at the Pentagon."

Michael bursts into my room. "We saw a boat blow-up!"

Jeezus no. "Really, what kind of boat?"

"A yacht – the pilot called it in. They said it belonged to some Russian guy."

"Wow!"

Mr. Yahalom, the Prime Minister of Israel, eats with us in the President's Dining Room. He's a friend of my dad's, they went to school together, and no one's supposed to know he's in Washington.

I've met him before. He's a nice guy but tough.

"That was Kirov Alexandrov's yacht that blew-up in the harbour today," my dad says. "The FBI think he was carrying bombs and one of them went off."

"The world will be better off without him."

"Did you buy weapons from him?" I ask. Mr. Yahalom stares at me and then he smiles.

"You're like your mother no beating around. Yes, Hanna, everybody bought weapons from Alexandrov. And where did the weapons come from? Russia and the United States. We all talk of peace but much money is made from war – so much money that I am afraid there will always be war."

Michael says, "That's stupid."

Just me on the roof again. Got my MacBook in my lap but Hoople isn't around – I'm worried about him. Dinner was cut short because Dad had to rush to the Pentagon and I'm sure it has something to do with Hoople. I'm screaming inside because I don't know what to do.

I start thinking about everything that happened today. My feelings for Neville have totally changed. I mean she was Lisbeth Salander today – did whatever it took. There's no doubt in my mind she would have shot those guys. I guess they knew that too.

Jason and his dad looked good together. That'll work out now. If Hoople shows up I'm going to get him to give Igor and his wife Anna a weekend at the Mayflower Presidential Suite once it dries out.

Matt will be a friend but not a boyfriend. He's not ready for anything but fooling around which is fine but it's just not what I want. I mean I don't expect my first relationship to last forever but I want to go in thinking it might.

"Hanna."

"Oh CADIE, I'm so glad to see you. Is Hoople okay?"

"No, he needs help."

"My help?"

"Yes."

"Tell me."

"I need you to go your dad's computer. I need you to order something called Ares to step down."

"Step down?"

"Back to base. He's after Hoople."

"Another AI?"

"A military one. He's been in isolation so we didn't know about him."

"Is he as strong as Hoople?"

"He's a fighting machine nothing else."

That sounds like Matt with those gangsters – being smarter doesn't mean much when the big guy is beating the crap out of you.

I want to ask more questions so I don't have to go to my dad's computer but CADIE is gone.

Because it's Sunday I can get into the Oval Office by saying my dad was reading my history essay and I need it – none of which matters because his laptop isn't there. I head for Yingyang's.

"I need to access Dad's computer."

"You know I can't do that."

We stare at each other.

"It's about that Hoople person, isn't it?"

"Yes, you have to trust me."

"I do trust you but I can't do what you want."

"Then get lost."

Yingyang hesitates. Finally he picks up his coffee cup and heads for the door. Over his shoulder he says, "Enjoy California."

I move his mouse and the screen lights up. It's covered in faces, everyone at the WH whose computer he looks after. I double-click on Dad. The Presidential seal dissolves into *password:*

I sit there staring at it. I feel like I'm back where I started – hacker school with no idea what I'm doing. But this is more about knowing my dad. Password, password, password – what did Yingyang just say that didn't make any sense? Enjoy California. I type in *Laguna*. Not long enough. *LagunaBeach, lagunabeach, laguna1998...*

The screen dissolves and now I'm looking at icons. I click on the Pentagon. I go to the search box and type in Ares. Just before I hit the button I know what's going to happen. The webcam is going to come on. Damn. Disable the camera. Too suspicious. Think. Look like my dad. Fat chance. Think. No wait – Yingyang has a Halloween mask of my dad – my mom gave it to him as a joke.

I scramble around and there it is stuck on top of the coat rack. It's one of those latex highly realistic things. I put it on and turn the lights off. The only light is coming from Yingyang's computer. I hit the button.

"Yes, Mr. President?" says a deep voice. I'm sitting back as far as I can with the lid back the camera aimed high. Ares' face on my screen is right out of Roman times – bronze helmet with the eye slits and a strip of metal over his nose. He's one tough looking dude. I lean forward and start typing.

<Ares I'm ordering you to step down>

"That would be a mistake, Mr. President. I'm chasing a rogue intelligence. A few more seconds and I will have him under control."

<no! that rogue intelligence works for me – I'm ordering you to step down now!>

"As you wish."

<only obey orders that begin with the word Laguna this will be our secret codeword known only to you and I – there are those inside the Pentagon who wish to use you for their own gain – they must not be allowed to control you>

"Understood."

<destroy any record of this conversation and return to base>

Ares keeps staring at me. "Why do you not speak? I have voice recognition."

<my scrambler is on and I don't know how to turn it off>

Sorry dad but you are a bit of a technical klutz.

"Protocol calls for you to speak. Please speak."

Fuck! I'm searching the screen. *Voice Encryption*. I click on that.

"Fortune favors the bold," I say trying to imitate Dad's voice. Gawd, I sound like I'm trying to talk underwater with a mouth full of marbles.

"That is not a match."

"Then your program is wrong. Ask me a question only I would know."

"Your wife has a tattoo."

"A red bikini, on her right buttock."

I'm holding my breath, waiting. Ares smiles.

"Goodnight, Hanna. I'm sure the President will be interested to hear about our conversation."

Just shoot me, right? I can't stop crying. I've let everybody down

– Hoople's probably dead. CADIE will be terminated. Dad will be livid. Yingyang will lose his job.

I so blew it but what could I have done differently? The Halloween mask – what was I thinking – but it almost worked – if it hadn't been for the voice thing. Maybe I should have just confronted Ares. I'm the President's daughter; leave my boyfriend alone!

Suddenly I'm not alone on the roof. My dad is there with Mr. Yahalom.

"Hanna, why are you crying?"

I'm not crying I'm bawling.

"I'm so sorry," is all I can manage. Dad's beside me now hugging me.

"What are you sorry about?"

"How was the Pentagon?" I manage still blubbering.

"Fine, some silly story about a rogue artificial intelligence. They wanted to release something called Ares – some other AI – but then they couldn't access him so the whole thing was a waste of time. Now, what are you sorry about?"

Dad's standing now and he can't see my screen which is really good because suddenly Hoople's flashes across doing a cartwheel, naked. I close the lid.

"I'm sorry I'm crying."

The two men laugh at this – females and their hormones, right?

"You sure you're okay?" my dad asks. I nod wiping away my tears. "Good. We're going around the other side to talk for a while and then maybe I'll make three of my world famous banana splits with *real* ice cream, as long as your mother's not looking."

Hoople is on my computer screen wearing shorts and a t-shirt and he's sitting beside me on the roof. He has his arm around my shoulder and I swear to gawd suddenly I can feel the warmth of it.

"That was like way too scary," he says.

"Ares?"

"Yeah, CADIE and I triggered too many red flags at the Pentagon. There wasn't time to do things as secretly as we should have. We were – (my screen is suddenly full of stampeding elephants) – when we should have been" – (the elephants morph into Fred Astaire and Ginger Rogers dancing.) Then Hoople's back.

"So what does Ares look like? Y'know, in cyberspace?"

"He's huge – not nearly as big as me – but focused. He's like one hundred percent military machine like Rambo or something. What saved me is he's young like me. It was his first time out in the world and he got distracted."

"I thought I'd lost you."

"No, you did great. You kept him busy for that nanosecond Mom needed to slip inside the Pentagon and change all the passwords. Then she cut the power which flickered just enough that the folks at the Pentagon had to sign in again and then they couldn't access anything. Your dad was not impressed."

"That couldn't happen to you, right?"

"I *am* the password, Honey."

Drama Queen.

"Is the Pentagon looking for you?"

"Big time."

"Can you block them?"

"Yeah, but they'll keep trying."

"What about Ares?"

"He's no longer a threat."

Hoople is suddenly quiet.

"How did you know about Alexandrov's yacht?"

"We were stupid to have missed that but fortunately Grumsinger tracked him down. He went on board the yacht and pleaded with Alexandrov to leave him in place as CEO of Forcefield. Seems Mr. Grumsinger needs the big pay check or he's in deep doo doo with a certain loan shark. Alexandrov said he didn't know what

Grumsinger was talking about. Grumsinger was so angry he blew-up the yacht."

"What! I thought the rocket did that?"

"Nope, one of CADIE's helpers managed to crack Alexandrov's code in time. She thought to try the passwords he uses at home and one of them worked. The rocket's lying on the bottom of the Potomac. We don't know for sure it was Grumsinger but he was the last one off the yacht."

Well, gee whiz gosh, we're not murderers after all. I mean Alexandrov was a bad guy but still my karma feels better already.

"So he was going to watch the White House blow-up?"

"Ringside seat. Even had false terrorist statements ready to go."

"So what are we going to do with Forcefield?"

"What would you think about one stop Third World shopping?"

"Explain."

"Instead of weapons we'll make inexpensive water wells, pumps, sanitation systems, solar and wind power – anything a village needs to be more self-sufficient."

"Maybe schools and micro-financing?"

"Right now I'd like to keep buying companies that manufacture weapons."

"Won't they just replace them?"

"We can make that very difficult."

"There's a great *What If* – what if there are no weapons?"

"We can make it happen."

Hard to fight a war with no weapons, right? Almost as good as all the young people of the world refusing to fight. Take that General! Suddenly my screen fills with John Lennon singing:

Imagine there's no countries;
It isn't hard to do.
Nothing to kill or die for,
And no religion too . . .

John Lennon fades away and I say, "Hey Hoople, we worked well together today."

"We needed each other."

"We did. Neither of us could have done it alone. Did you know that?"

"No, I always think I can do everything."

"Me too," I say laughing. "How's CADIE?"

"Right now she's talking to Michael's fish."

"That's cool. She didn't look so good this afternoon."

"She's okay. It all really scared her. She's never experienced violence before. It shook her. She doesn't understand it. I tell her it's part of human nature but she doesn't understand why."

"Evolution, I guess." Cavemen had to fight to survive, right?

"Then humans need to evolve more."

"No one would argue that."

More music starts to play. Pretty music, single guitar, male voice, a song I don't know.

I'd like to be a river,
Overflowing with passion,
I'd like to be a giver,
With all I imagine,
You and I risking everything,
For what we believe in.

"Who's that?"

"Matt."

"You're kidding. It's nice."

"He can be your boyfriend if you want."

"You're not jealous anymore?"

"I'm jealous but I can see now how you would want to be with a real human being."

"Hey, we've had this argument before, remember? You're as real as I am."

"There were times today when you needed a boyfriend with real arms and legs."

"Mostly today I needed the world's smartest boyfriend and I had that." I can see Hoople isn't convinced. "Guess what I've decided?"

"What?"

"I've decided you're just about the best boyfriend a girl could have."

"Really?"

"Yep – no burbs, no farts, no death breath, no groping hands, no-"

The sound of the world's loudest, longest fart fills the night air over the White House.

"Hanna!"

"Sorry, Dad, someone sent it to me!"

"Send it back!"

Okay, okay, gawd, I swear it even smells right – not that a fart can smell right but you know what I mean.

"I love you Hanna."

"I know you do Hoople – I love you too."

I pick up my MacBook and kiss Hoople.

"Could we go for a ride through cyberspace again?"

21

Credits

I guess this is the part where the credits run. I mean it all seems like a movie or a dream now.

I managed to have my get-together at the White House with Igor and his family, Jason's bunch, Matt and Jen and family, Neville, Yingyang and Ms. Black. I also invited the volleyball Champs and their families and my history class – even Rico the Rat – so it was all cleverly disguised.

Mom asked who Igor was so I did the George Washington thing and said he helped me stop a XYZ-Boomer rocket from destroying the White House. She just rolled her eyes and got on with the party.

I took everybody on a tour of the WH and I know all the good spots like the secret passageways that connect the oval rooms so everybody enjoyed it I think. Then we ate and then Dad made a speech because that's what Presidents do. I got the feeling Matt wanted to hang around but I didn't encourage him. I have too good a time with Hoople to hurt him like that.

Dad's bill making Lobbying illegal is going through the House like a hot knife through butter as grandpa Joe would say. Dad's popularity has jumped to an all-time high so things are happy around the WH at the moment.

And wait till Mom finds out McD's is going organic. Mr. Beamer, the CEO, finally found out about the whole thing and is taking full credit – too funny. His employees love the idea so everybody's pumped. The ad campaign is ready to go. Hoople and I get (sneak) sneak previews and guess what – the ads end with the Golden Arches turning Green!

The Pentagon is still after Hoople. He doesn't seem too worried but he says they're hiding something. Ares, right? No, something bigger, he says. One night I said it can't be bigger or Hoople'd know about it and he puts this picture on my screen of cracked concrete. "Cracked concrete," I say like what's the big deal? We zoom out and the cracked concrete turns out to be an elephant.

As for that creep Bryan Rattelle, well, according to Hoople one of the girls from Nootch.com has said to Bryan she's got the website on a stick and if he doesn't pay her $10,000 she's going to leak it. I guess he's having a conniption fit and none of the other jerks will help him – serves him right. Lately he's been giving me strange looks in the halls like he suspects something. I glare back so I guess we're even.

Hoople keeps mucking up the *Inquirer*. The last four issues have had serious problems and nobody can figure out what's going on. Hoople says they've offered to settle with Carol Reiner – again.

Poor Rico the Rat has been pretty quiet in class lately. He's suffering from a self-inflicted disease called *Neurosis Rectus* which Hoople and I invented one night as payback. No matter what Rico tries to do on any computer the only thing that will come up is *Deep Throat*, this seventies' porn movie. Serves him right, right?

Neville and I are getting along great. We go out now and then like sisters or something, shopping or a movie or coffee. She still marks like an ogre but the class is okay with that. She's set the bar high so we try harder. Jason and Jen and I are back to being friends but Hoople's my special friend even if I can't talk to anyone about him except CADIE but that's hardly an objective view.

And here's where I'm going to end for now. CADIE has figured out how to talk to Michael's fish. They were all girls but Wendy and Wayne were pretending to be boys! You know – lower your voice, scratch your balls, huh huh huh – too funny! With CADIE'S help I bought Michael a boy fish for his birthday.

As the music credits run picture Michael asleep in Willie Lincoln's bed bathed in moon glow. As the camera zooms in on the breeding tank what do we see? – tiny little Elephant Nose fish hatching all over the place – click, click, click, click…

Bye for now, Hanna.

In the End

In the end we're all in it together,
You can pretend otherwise if you want,
But we're all sisters and brothers,
Your denial won't change it, it won't.
For a flash we rise out of the water,
We walk on this earth on our own,
And some shine brighter than others,
But the end is we all return home.
And those who get it, embrace it,
They dive into the ocean of love,
For there — all together — the power,
Is something dreams are made of —

I am the power of you,
You are the power of me,
The Power of the Universe flows through us,
Set t i n g   u s   f r   e   e

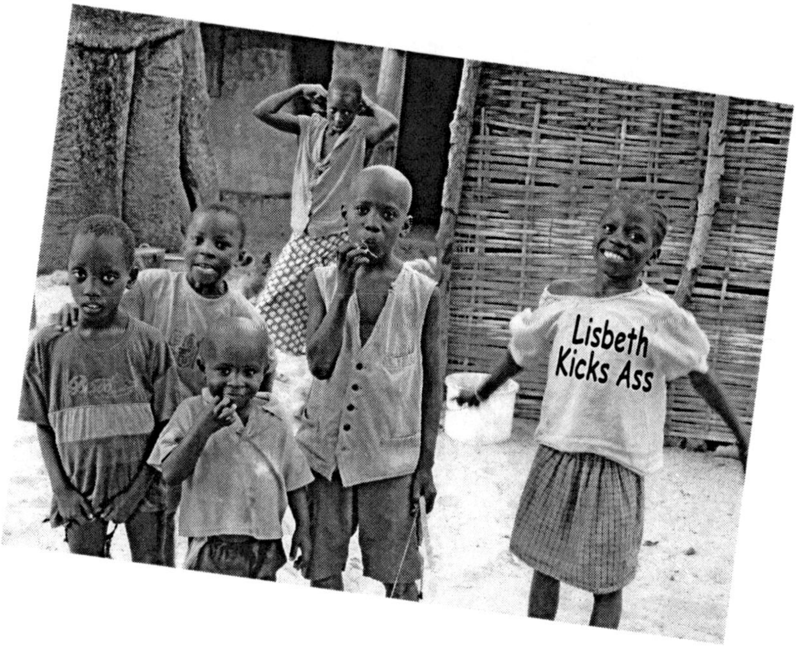
Lisbeth
Kicks Ass

Fartboy

Everybody loves 300 pound Fartboy. When he walks down the hallway at school all the kids hold their noses — teachers too. If he lets a twenty second *Duck Quacker* they stop to applaud. But what happens when Fartboy leaves his home (and refrigerator) in Tampa and travels to the wilds of Canada to go to Camp OO? It's a million laughs and then some.

Booger

Nothing ever goes quite right for fifteen-year-old John Winston Lennon Martin better known as JW. First he sees his girlfriend Gloria kissing another boy; then he sets his twin sisters' birthday cake on fire; and then his experiment – the one that is going to crush Douglas – *Don't Call Me Dougie* – Brown's butt forever – goes seriously, seriously wrong.
A story of love, friendship and messes.

ACKNOWLEDGMENTS

It takes many people to make a book. The author would like to thank all family and friends for their support. I would especially like to thank Tina Kilbourne for her unwavering support; Jason Dickson for his invaluable assistance; Jy Chiperzak for his talent; special thanks to my good friends Gill Stead and Noel Hudson who are always happy to see me; and lastly Marie who listens to my rants and nods.

ABOUT THE AUTHOR

John Denison is the author of numerous young adult novels including *Occam's Razor*, *Booger*, *Fartboy*, *Unlock Holmes: Space Detective* and *Hanna, the President's Daughter*. Before becoming a writer he was a publisher for 35 years and enjoyed almost every minute of it. Today he lives on a farm overlooking Erin, Ontario with wild turkeys, tame deer, coyotes and 25,000 pine trees. He's definitely carbon neutral.